"Your heart is beating a hundred miles an hour," Adam said.

Molly couldn't deny it.

"Come inside," he offered. "I'll make coffee. We're both spooked."

"I left the dog alone, and my house is wide-open." Molly didn't think she could go into the small tack room where he was staying. Where the only place to sit would be on Adam's rumpled bed. "I had coffee with my friend Tess. More caffeine this late would keep me up all night. I'm fine. Really. I don't think there's a cricket stirring tonight."

"All the same, let me put on my boots. I'll walk you back to the house. It's dark, and the barn lights and your porch light don't reach into the shadows."

"Okay." She rubbed away goose bumps from her upper arms as Adam turned away. "And maybe put on a shirt," she added feebly.

Dear Reader,

Book ideas come from so many different places. This one seeped into my head little by little, from a variety of sources. I'm a big clipper of newspaper articles. I cut a couple from our Sunday paper about some new farm-to-fork gardens that involved children in the planting process. The idea was that they'd learn to like vegetables after helping to grow a garden. At the same time that I saw those articles, I watched a documentary on TV about child hunger in the US and how schools are collecting food from area grocers to send home in backpacks so kids and their families have food over a weekend. I learned this is happening in my area schools, and our community food bank is desperate for more help feeding hungry families.

Molly McNair came into my head as someone who loves to garden and wanted to fill a need. Another article mentioned that crop yields around here are plummeting as more land is used to explore for fossil fuels. So I had Molly's conflict but needed to find her a suitable hero. Adam Hollister appeared as a contender. He has the background to cause Molly trouble. But nice guy that he is, he recognizes that what she's doing to help poor families survive is more important than his former friends drilling for more oil. Oh, and Molly has a dog, a Doberman, that Adam wins over, too. I hope you like the good times I've given this couple (and that you enjoy seeing them triumph over the bad ones!).

Sincerely,

Roz Denny Fox

Email: rdfox@cox.net

HEARTWARMING

Molly's Garden

—

Roz Denny Fox

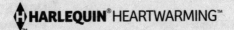
HARLEQUIN® HEARTWARMING™

Recycling programs
for this product may
not exist in your area.

ISBN-13: 978-0-373-36736-8

Molly's Garden

Copyright © 2015 by Rosaline Fox

All rights reserved. Except for use in any review, the reproduction or utilization of this work in whole or in part in any form by any electronic, mechanical or other means, now known or hereinafter invented, including xerography, photocopying and recording, or in any information storage or retrieval system, is forbidden without the written permission of the publisher, Harlequin Enterprises Limited, 225 Duncan Mill Road, Don Mills, Ontario M3B 3K9, Canada.

This is a work of fiction. Names, characters, places and incidents are either the product of the author's imagination or are used fictitiously, and any resemblance to actual persons, living or dead, business establishments, events or locales is entirely coincidental.

This edition published by arrangement with Harlequin Books S.A.

For questions and comments about the quality of this book, please contact us at CustomerService@Harlequin.com.

® and TM are trademarks of Harlequin Enterprises Limited or its corporate affiliates. Trademarks indicated with ® are registered in the United States Patent and Trademark Office, the Canadian Intellectual Property Office and in other countries.

Printed in U.S.A.

Roz Denny Fox's first book was published by Harlequin in 1990. She writes for several Harlequin lines and for special projects. Her books are published worldwide and in a number of languages. She's also written articles as well as online serials for Harlequin.com. Roz's warm home-and-family-focused love stories have been nominated for various industry awards, including the Romance Writers of America's RITA® Award, the Holt Medallion, the Golden Quill and others. Roz has been a member of the Romance Writers of America since 1987 and is currently a member of Tucson's Saguaro Romance Writers, where she has received the Barbara Award for outstanding chapter service. In 2013 Roz received her fifty-book pin from Harlequin. Readers can email her through Facebook or at rdfox@cox.net, or visit her website at korynna.com/RozFox.

Books by Roz Denny Fox

HARLEQUIN HEARTWARMING

Hearts Entwined
The Western Dare
The Boss Next Door
The Hope Dress
Annie's Neighborhood
An Unlikely Rancher

HARLEQUIN AMERICAN ROMANCE

The Secret Wedding Dress
The Perfect Tree
The Maverick Returns
Duke: Deputy Cowboy
Texas Dad
Texas Mom

Visit the Author Profile page
at Harlequin.com for more titles.

To Paula Eykelhof, the dedicated, insightful editor who catches my goofs and makes my books better with her expertise. A mere thank-you will never be enough.

CHAPTER ONE

MOLLY MCNAIR TIGHTENED her grip on Nitro's leash and charged up the steps. Bursting through the double doors into the sheriff's station, she stood looking for Deputy Roy Powell.

A uniformed clerk set down the phone, eyeing her big guard dog warily. "May I help you?"

The woman stepped out from behind her desk and the black-and-rust Doberman growled low in his throat. The clerk immediately retreated.

"I got a message from Deputy Powell. Ramon Flores was in some kind of an accident. He was driving one of our McNair trucks to markets in Laredo."

The woman turned as Roy Powell, in his khaki uniform, emerged from a back room and signaled with a hand. "Park your dog outside and come with me, Ms. McNair."

Molly tightened her grip on Nitro. "My dog stays with me, if you don't mind, Deputy Powell."

She spoke a low command and the animal relaxed.

"Then see he behaves." Powell went into the room and waited for her.

She stepped past him and pulled up short. "Ramon. Good grief, what happened?"

Her driver sat hunched over in a straight-backed chair. His hair was matted with blood. One eye was nearly closed and beginning to bruise. His shirt and pants were torn and dirty. Fresh blood oozed from several cuts on his arm and through one pant leg.

"Why is he here and not at the hospital?" Molly asked Powell, who'd gone to sit behind his desk. Nitro sniffed at Ramon and sat. She remained standing.

"Mr. Flores told officers at the scene that he wasn't sure he had a medical policy. He has no identification. Frankly we contacted you, as the registered owner of the vehicle, not knowing whether he'd stolen your truck."

"Ramon, where's your driver's license?" She turned to Powell. "I provide all employees an insurance card."

Looking miserable, Ramon continued to clutch his ribs as he spoke. "Three men in a black SUV forced me off the road before I reached the highway. They pulled me out of the cab. One beat me while the others destroyed the crates…and the produce inside. One took my wallet."

Molly gaped at him. "He plainly needs medical treatment. What do I have to do for you to release him so I can take him to the emergency room? Or, Ramon, do you need me to call an ambulance?"

He shook his head even as the deputy drummed his thumbs on a manila folder. "Can you prove he's in Texas legally?"

"Prove? Ramon's parents migrated from Mexico a long time ago. Daddy helped them become naturalized. And you know my father was a straight arrow." Her voice trembled as she spoke and Nitro sat up. Reaching down, she stroked between his pointed ears.

"It's been a year since your dad passed. A lot has changed. Rumors say you aren't as choosey about who you hire as Mike was."

"What? That's not true. Daddy supported me and all the farm decisions I had to make after he got prostate cancer. I've been at this long enough now…why are there suddenly questions? I was in the Peace Corps, for crying out loud, doesn't that warrant some kind of respect for my decision-making?"

"Raising cattle is a worthy occupation. Your dad's wranglers were mostly local cowboys." The deputy delivered a dark look as he closed the folder. "You should have stuck with raising beef."

Molly stiffened. "Meaning you don't think providing fresh fruit and vegetables to hungry families is admirable?"

"Depends on who you're feeding. You don't want to be encouraging people to come here who don't belong."

"You know what? None of that matters. This man works for me. He belongs and he needs a doctor. I'm taking him to the hospital. If you plan to detain us, I'll phone Gordon Loomis."

Molly pulled out her cell phone. Loomis, her godfather, was the most respected lawyer in the area. His name carried weight. He'd been their family attorney even before Molly's mom died. And she had few memories of her mother.

"Out of curiosity, are you looking for the men who did this?" she abruptly asked.

Powell stood. "I don't need you to tell me my job, little lady. Your produce truck might've been hijacked by the very folks you've been feeding. Maybe you should sell your farm and go back to your old job in... where was that again?" he drawled. *"Africa?"*

"You mean where we were treated with respect?" Pocketing her phone, Molly dealt the deputy a dirty look. Shifting Nitro's leash to her left hand, she leaned down to help her driver to his feet. "I'll send someone from the farm to collect my truck to see if we can salvage any of the load. I assume you have no reason to hold it."

"If you have known enemies, Ms. McNair, I'll take their names. The mischief-makers were gone by the time a passerby phoned our dispatch."

Molly indicated Ramon's injuries. "This looks like more than mischief to me."

"A lot of old-timers hate the influx streaming across our border. You ought'a be extra careful about who you put on your payroll. I'll be checking."

Ignoring the arrogance of the paunchy deputy, Molly slowly led her driver out of the office, through the main room, which had fallen silent, and out the door.

"I'm sorry I couldn't save the vegetables." Ramon spoke with effort. "I think one man was the same one I told you hassled me at the market on Monday." He faltered and she stopped to steady him. "I can't be your driver anymore," he said slowly, staring down at his feet. "Elena worries. And we have three children. You pay me more to drive, but I'll go back to hoeing or picking... They threatened to hurt my family."

She took a sharp breath before nudging him forward again. "None of this makes sense. Why would anyone be so upset that I'm selling fresh vegetables at local farmers' markets?"

Frowning, Molly unlocked the doors to

her old SUV. She removed Nitro's leash and he bounded into the backseat. Carefully she helped Ramon into the front passenger's seat.

"I don't want to get dirt and blood on your upholstery."

"This is a working farm vehicle. The seats will come clean. I'm sorry this happened. I should have paid closer attention when Danny Ortega quit. To be honest, he griped about everything so I assumed he'd finally had enough or had heard they were hiring in Brownsville for an offshore oil rig that paid more. Maybe he was being harassed, too."

She circled around, climbed in and started the motor. "You don't suppose the guys who jumped you were FDA vigilantes or food safety activists? I've complied with the new rules of organic agriculture. We even installed water filters to the irrigation that the government won't require until next year."

She knew the FDA had become more aggressive in its inspections. But what grower wanted to sell tainted food? She'd gotten her degree in agriculture because she wanted to

grow crops that helped families be healthier. It had been her main mission in going
to Africa.

At the hospital, she found a shady spot
and parked. Again assisting Ramon, she
rolled the windows down a few inches and
told Nitro to stay. The hospital only allowed
service dogs inside. But the sun was wan-
ing and a nice spring breeze had sprung up.
Later, when summer arrived, she wouldn't
be able to leave him in the vehicle.

The emergency waiting area overflowed
with moms and crying children. Molly
found Ramon a seat and then went to the
counter to check him in. A harried clerk
gave her a clipboard with a sheaf of papers,
which she handed to Ramon to fill out while
she phoned her insurance agent.

"Lawrence, Molly McNair. I have an employee in the emergency waiting room." She
quickly explained the situation, including
the news about Ramon's missing insurance
card, and was advised to pay the bill and
the agent would arrange for reimbursement.

"Do you happen to know anyone looking for a truck-driving job?" she asked Law-

rence. "Someone big and burly? Or, failing that, someone proficient in martial arts?" She laughed, but there was truth in her statement.

"You need to work with the police, Molly. And be extra careful. Last time I visited your dad, Mike was concerned about you being left alone out there."

"Dad carped on that," she said, a smile in her voice.

"I understand why he'd worry. The ranch is about as remote as they come. Considering the increase in Rio Grande crossings… well, it's dangerous for anyone alone."

"Rather than lasso a husband, Lawrence, I got a Doberman."

The man chuckled. "I'm just saying, when jobs get scarce some men get aggressive. I hope Roy Powell finds who ran your driver off the—" He broke off, then added, "Listen, I have a call coming in on another line. I'll have my secretary see to Mr. Flores's replacement card."

"Thanks." Molly clicked off and went back to Ramon, picking up the clipboard from the empty seat beside him. Looking at him for permission, he nodded, and she quickly scanned the paperwork. Uncapping the pen, she filled in the lines Ramon had left blank, showing him before returning it to the clerk.

Back in her seat, she called the farm to ask Henry Garcia, her dad's long-standing ranch manager, to drive another of her hands out in the Jeep to collect the delivery truck. "Henry, see if there's anything salvageable of the load. Maybe there's stuff we can give to the food bank."

She hesitated before adding, "Watch yourselves."

She signed off and idly picked up a tattered magazine. She tried to think what next steps she could take to keep what had happened to Ramon from happening again. She remained at a loss as to why anyone would do such a thing.

While he was being examined, Molly stepped outside to call the weekly newspaper to place an ad for an experienced truck driver. She added a line about having to be able to heft fifty-pound crates. A crate rarely weighed that much, but maybe it would net her a brawny guy capable of holding his own against miscreants.

Going back inside, she sat again until Ramon came out of the examining room.

"The doctor didn't find any bad injuries. He cleaned my cuts and gave me an antibiotic cream. He says I should do light duty for a week because my ribs are bruised."

"I'm glad it's not worse." Molly paid with her farm credit card and they left.

They didn't talk much on the drive.

As she dropped Ramon off at his house, she said, "Plan on potting in the greenhouses until you heal. Once you're better you can join the irrigation crew where you'll make a little more money."

"I'll work hard at whatever you want me to do."

"I know that, Ramon."

TWO DAYS LATER the newspaper with her ad came out and Molly alerted Henry to take phone numbers from interested applicants.

But for three days no one called. Busy harvesting lettuce, Swiss chard, radishes and bush beans, and with spring weather warming and ripening the tomatoes, Molly, who disliked driving the flatbed, packed her

SUV and made extra trips to the markets. She took Nitro and remained vigilant. Luckily there were no incidents.

By Wednesday of the following week she'd only talked to two candidates. Both unsuitable. She began to worry that she'd blown it with the weight requirement…and had been too quick to dismiss those applicants. Although one had had no references and the other had been fired from his previous job for drinking, clearly thinking that wouldn't come up in a reference check.

Thursday morning, as she prepared to go to a market in Carrizo Springs, Molly noticed a well-dressed man talking to a field hand in a newly plowed area earmarked for local students: a planting program she'd established for third-graders from two low-income schools.

"Henry, who's the guy talking to Rick?"

The manager stepped out of the barn. "I don't know. I saw him a couple of weeks ago walking the spinach rows. I thought from his clothes he was an inspector."

"And you didn't think to tell me that?"

She stripped off her gloves and snapped her fingers to rouse Nitro from his snooze.

"I know all the food safety inspectors," she said, clipping on the dog's leash. The man in question wore pants, a short-sleeved shirt and a tie. She saw him squat and sift dirt through one hand. "Considering what happened to Ramon, I don't like strangers wandering my land."

It only took her a couple of minutes to cross the field and come up on the man from behind.

Nitro began to growl.

The stranger sprang up, dusted off his hands and backed away.

Molly delivered a hand command to Nitro, but the big dog strained at his leash.

"May I ask what you are doing? I'm Molly McNair. I own this land."

"You grow some fine-looking vegetables. Good soil, I assume?"

"Very. Are you a state inspector?"

"Nope." The man stepped farther away from Nitro.

"I don't sell direct to the public." She named a few farmers' markets. "You can find us there. I open for U-pick at the end of harvest."

The man said nothing.

"I see a Humvee parked up on the main highway. Most visitors drive through our gate and down the lane. I'll ask again... Who are you?"

Molly had learned from her years in the Peace Corps to judge friend and foe quickly. She absorbed the stranger's toothy smile, noting it didn't reach his cold blue eyes.

He dug a business card out of his shirt pocket and extended it—jerking back his hand when Nitro bared his teeth.

"Settle, Nitro."

Molly picked up the fallen card and was surprised that it had nothing on it about farm implements, fertilizers or any possible outlet for her wares.

"Branchville Oil? Not what I expected. That's a group my dad wanted nothing to do with."

"I'm a new subcontractor. I understand they tried to buy mineral rights from Mr. McNair. Branchville is on the hunt for new oil fields in South Texas. If you still hold those rights—" he motioned one hand in a circle "—I'm prepared to offer you a fair sum to let the company sink a dozen or so small test holes. It's lucrative income for doing nothing on your part. If I find oil, we'll bargain for significantly more money."

Molly tried to pass back his card, but his hands were now in his pockets.

"I've no interest in letting anyone search for fossil fuel on my land. The answer is no."

The man's jaw tensed.

"Your name is…?" Molly persisted. "There's none on this business card."

"Think the offer over. When you're ready to deal, call the number at the bottom. A few pumping oil wells will earn you a lot more than slaving over crops that depend on many more variables."

"Such as?"

"Drought. Floods. Tornadoes."

She stared at the man for a moment before he turned and walked away.

Molly watched him weave through her field of pole beans and up the bank to the black Humvee, where he got in and quickly drove off.

Only then did Nitro settle.

Henry materialized at Molly's elbow. "What did he want? Did he say why he didn't come in through the main gate?"

Giving a half laugh, she showed Henry the card. "He's a man with no name who wants to dig test wells in the middle of my crops."

The old man took the card in a gnarled brown hand. His eyes remained on the road. "Your papa thought you should fence along the highway. Maybe it's time."

"Maybe." Molly strode out of the empty field to her SUV. "Right now I have produce to deliver."

ADAM HOLLISTER FINISHED setting up a row of clean pilsner glasses and gave the glazed oak counter a last wipe before he opened the bar. It was midweek. He didn't expect much traffic other than the few regulars who stopped by after work.

He straightened stools on his way to put out the Open sign. Heading back, he plugged some coins into the jukebox and again stood behind the bar as Miranda Lambert belted out her latest he-done-me-wrong song.

Catching a glimpse of his image in the leaded mirror on the wall behind the liquor bottles, Adam barely recognized the man he saw. He'd let his hair, once clipped short, curl to his shoulders. He'd taken to wearing a headband to hold it out of his eyes. He should probably shave more often, he thought, stroking his prickly cheek.

He might be a bit gaunt, but this lazy job working the Country-Western bar for his old college friend in the dusty outskirts of Catarina, Texas, hadn't diminished his six-three stature or turned the muscles that he'd honed over his years as a wildcatter flabby. His imposing size was probably why Frank had begged him to manage the bar he'd inherited from his father in the rough border town.

One look and few, if any, messed with Adam Hollister.

The door opened. Two regulars walked in and took seats at the far end of the bar. One held up two fingers and Adam pulled two dark ales from the tap. No words passed between them as he delivered their drinks.

Three old-timers Adam knew by sight wandered in next and ordered. They opted for a booth near the jukebox. They fed the machine and Willie Nelson crooned a series of his old hits.

Predictable, Adam thought, wiping at a nonexistent spill. Weeknights were dead. He hoped Frank finished renovating his dad's old house soon, so Adam could quit this place.

The door swung open again. As was his habit, Adam looked up. He did a double-take and was more than a little shocked to recognize Dave Benson.

His former business partner strolled up to the bar and took a stool in front of him.

The last time Adam had seen Dave had been at Jenny and Lindy's funerals.

A pain that never quite went away stabbed him anew. He'd tried running away from that memory, that pain, that guilt, for more than two years.

"You look like something the cat dragged in," Dave said.

"Thanks. What brings you slumming? You still drink light beer?"

Benson made a rude gesture before admitting he hadn't changed his preference. "I've been looking for you, good buddy. Jim Stafford's secretary finally broke down and told me where to find you. Kevin Cole wouldn't give me the time of day."

Adam popped the top on a bottle and watched as Dave took a long swallow. This was the man Adam had entrusted with his thriving multimillion dollar company, Hollister-Benson Wildcatters.

Dave wore a white shirt and tie—so out of place here.

"Why are you hunting for me? Didn't Cole, Cole and Stafford cross all the T's to make the company transfer legal?"

"They did. Although it sticks in Kevin's craw that you gave me the company." Dave tore a loose piece of label from the bottle and wadded it into a tiny ball he dropped in the ashtray. "Business has been slow. Then two months ago I got a call from a guy we did a job for in Kuwait. He's a new partner in Branchville Oil, based out of Corpus. It seems the government is offering big-buck contracts to anyone who can open up rich new in-ground veins. If you've watched any global news lately, you know the foreign oil markets are stagnant. Domestic is the way to make a killing."

"I don't watch much news." Adam stepped away to get refills for the two at the end of the bar. "How does any of that affect me?" he asked on his return.

"Branchville had a chemist do soil studies for them last year. He thinks there could be a major field below a ranch not far from here."

"So?" Adam leaned back against the bar sink and crossed his arms.

"Ranch owner refused to sell the mineral rights or to allow testing. He died and left the property to an equally stubborn woman. I talked to her yesterday. She's as anti-oil as the old man was."

"Tough for you. Sounds like you've hit a brick wall, Dave."

"That's why I thought of you. This could mean millions, and you have a sixth sense when it comes to making sure there's oil and talking people out of it."

"Money doesn't mean squat to me now. I made more than I'll ever need and I was wrong to let it dictate my life."

"Well, even if you're not interested in personal profit, think of doing it for your country. Help wean the good old US of A off foreign oil."

Adam considered Dave's words. Perhaps thirty months was too long to wallow in self-pity. Oil definitely used to spark an adrenaline rush for him. "This isn't the most stimulating job. But if the landowner won't allow testing, that's pretty final."

Dave pulled a folded piece of newspaper out of his pocket. "Maybe there's another way. This morning the big boss at Branchville gave me this ad. The woman in question first ran it a week ago. Apparently the job hasn't been filled."

Taking the paper, Adam read the ad. "You could do this. Why don't you apply?"

"I spoke with her, so she knows me. She's not stupid, just stubborn. We hear she's not well liked in the area. Not by some townsfolk at least. Word is she makes life easy for border crossers. Authorities haven't caught her hiring or hiding illegals, but she's a sympathizer. At the local café I found out she supplies crossers with food and water."

"Why get in the middle of a hostile nego-tiation, Dave?"

"For a spanking-new oil supply."

Adam pursed his lips and read the ad again. "Maybe I don't qualify. Anyway, if she's a hard-nose like you suggest, if she caught me testing her dirt she'd probably fire me on the spot or toss my body in the Rio Grande."

Dave took another swig from the bottle. "You're complaining to a guy who's seen you charm your way out of many a hot spot, friend. I can tell you're interested. Of course, I trust you have a barber."

"Hmm. How would you figure to play this? I've no desire to work for Branchville or to renew my ties to Hollister-Benson Wildcatters. If I'm hired by the woman I'd want to remain unencumbered. Say I take a gander? It's gotta be at my pace and above-board. No pressure from you or your people.

If she refuses to deal, I walk away regardless."

Dave circled his sweating beer bottle around and around in circles of condensation, frowning all the while.

"What's the matter? That's my offer. Take it or leave it."

"It's just that the government offer runs out the first of July. That's what—six weeks? Not a lot of time. It also occurs to me Branchville might be uneasy if you don't have any skin in the game. I mean, your name is synonymous with the best wildcatter in the world. My bosses will want assurances you won't undercut them and blow in a well on your own."

Picking up the rag he'd used earlier to polish the bar, Adam wiped up the rings under Dave's bottle and shoved the empty into the return crate. "I'm not signing any contract except for a W-4 tax form if the farm owner hires me. It's your call."

His one-time partner stared at Adam for what seemed like a long time. Finally he muttered, "Give me a napkin. I'll draw a map to McNair Gardens. That's what she calls it. Used to be McNair Cattle Ranch."

"I'll find it. And write down a phone number where I can get in touch with you if I decide it's worth drilling there. Your people have nothing but the word of a chemist. They're known to be wrong. Or maybe you've forgotten the sheikh who bet a fortune on such a report and we drilled what turned out to be a duster."

"I remember you tried to tell him and he wouldn't listen. There are a number of people at Branchville who think the chemist is right." Dave scribbled a phone number on a clean bar napkin and slid it across to Adam. "Do you have to give notice here? I'd hate for someone to beat you to that truck-driving job."

"It's not a problem. I'll mosey on over there tomorrow and decide if I want to quit here."

As if he knew he'd pressed hard enough, Dave slid off the stool and hitched up his pants. "By the way, I don't recommend snooping around much in advance. The woman owns a killer dog. The Doberman didn't bite me, but only because she held him in check. Good luck, buddy. I'll touch base later."

Adam let Dave go without further response. He stared at the raggedly torn-out ad and the scribbled phone number on the napkin. His drive to become a multimillionaire had lost him Jenny and Lindy, the two most precious things in his life. He'd let chasing after big bucks mean more than his family. The money still sat untapped—where it could stay.

Dave might be betting on the wrong man, though, Adam thought. He'd been out of the oil business for more than two years. Admittedly it had once been his life. Work he'd chosen at seventeen. Next week he'd turn forty-one.

But he couldn't resist the lure of the hunt. For old times' sake he'd have a look-see at McNair Gardens.

Looking around the bar, he knew he owed Frank a lot for this job. Frank had seen Adam's reckless attitude toward life. Good friend that he was, Adam knew Frank would understand his desire to help out a former partner.

After seeing to the old-timers' refills, he picked up the phone.

"I figured this day would come," Frank Tully said. "I'm grateful you stuck around and helped out for as long as you did while I renovated the house. Diane said it's time I get behind the bar, anyway. But, listen, if you go over there and don't want to get involved, there's still a job here for you. We'll work something out. I told you my dad used to bring in live music on weekends. I'd like to do that again. It's bound to draw crowds, so I'll need help with control if nothing else."

"I appreciate your friendship. I'll take a run over there tomorrow. If the woman hires me, I'll still need to rent your travel trailer, if I may."

"Sure. She'd be stupid to not hire you. On the other hand, bud, you may want to lose the scruff."

"I'll shave and maybe get my hair trimmed. But why get gussied up?" Adam laughed. "Oh, one other favor. Will you provide a reference? Just don't mention my past work."

Adam finished out the night at the bar, all the while his mind straying ahead to hunting for oil again.

THE FULL-THROATED growl of a motorcycle roaring down her laneway jarred Molly from her task at hand. She stood from where she'd been kneeling among two dozen or so third-graders.

"That's a cool Harley," one big-eyed boy said. "My uncle had one, but it got stoled," he added when Molly took her eyes off the biker to glance down at him.

She signaled one of her teacher helpers. "Callie, would you help them finish this row of carrots? If I'm not back by the time you finish, start on those flats of sugar peas. There's enough for two long rows."

"He looks yummy from a distance," Grace, a teacher, added with a grin.

"Hmm," was Molly's response.

Removing her gloves, she tucked them under a sisal belt that held up her ragged jeans.

She stepped out of the raised bed and collected Nitro who'd been dozing in the shade afforded by one of several pecan trees that had been on the property since Molly had played here as a child.

The Doberman seemed to like the kids.

Adults were a different matter.

"Hello?" Molly called out to the stranger, who'd gone into the barn but then come out and gotten on his bike.

HEARING A SHOUT, Adam paused. He noticed a woman standing at the edge of a newly plowed field. She was a distance away, which gave him time to assess her and the monster dog Dave had mentioned, which hugged her side as she approached.

If she was the current property owner, she was younger than Adam had expected. Slender and willowy, she had a fresh-scrubbed face capped by curly hair, black as a moonless night sky. As shiny and black as her dog's coat. And her gardens were more extensive than he'd pictured.

What gave him the biggest start was seeing she had young children working in raised dirt beds. Did she employ child labor?

The sound of laughing youngsters hit him like a punch to his gut. The kids looked to be about the age his daughter Lindy would be.

Last month she would have turned seven.

MOLLY STOPPED WELL short of the man seated astride his motorcycle like a cowboy sat his horse. Up close he looked big and brash in his threadbare jeans and motorcycle boots.

Edging nearer, she saw her own hesitant self in mirrored sunglasses he had yet to remove and she shivered. He held a helmet, wearing a narrow red, white and blue headband that held back taffy-blond hair curling around his ears and collar. He reminded her of a young Brett Michaels, and that wasn't a bad image.

"I'm Molly McNair. May I help you?" She watched him unsnap a pearl button on the breast pocket of a blue Western-style shirt. She blinked as he extended a piece of paper.

The action was enough to make Nitro do something he'd never done before. He jerked his leash right out of Molly's grasp and bounded up to the Harley.

She made a grab for him and missed. The next thing that happened was more shocking.

The man, who had yet to identify himself, stripped off his sunglasses with one hand and reached down with the other, murmuring soothingly until the dog dropped to the ground. Nitro rolled onto his back and wriggled in the dirt as the man laughed and scratched his exposed belly.

Molly's jaw dropped. Impressed but wary, she crossed to the biker and took back her traitorous pet's leash. It was then she saw the paper that had fluttered from the man's hand. Her ad, torn from the newspaper. Bending, she picked it up.

"I came about the driver's position." The biker twirled his sunglasses by one arm. "Has the job been filled?"

Molly's cell phone rang and she answered it before replying. It was Henry. He'd seen the man ride down the lane. "Are you okay?" he asked. "I'm two minutes away."

"I'm fine. He's an applicant for the job. Yes, I see you at the barn now. Good. I need to get back to the students. I'll leave you to give him an application."

"Okay." Henry disconnected.

"My manager, Henry Garcia, has applications in the barn office." She gestured toward the children in the field. "My class awaits."

"By the way, I'm Adam Hollister," the man said. He bent and gave Nitro a last few head rubs before climbing off the bike and striding toward where Henry waited.

Molly silently watched him leave. He certainly looked as if he could stand up for himself.

For the farm.

Still, she wondered about the newcomer. Adam Hollister. His eyes, more gray than blue, had roamed over her with disturbing ease. Unless that was her imagination...

Certainly the way he'd made friends with Nitro left her feeling jittery.

She wasn't one to be smitten by the way a

man looked. She'd grown up around good-looking cowboys. And she'd worked with a wide range of men in the Peace Corps.

Nothing had quite piqued her curiosity or affected her equilibrium as quickly as this brief encounter with Adam Hollister.

CHAPTER TWO

MOLLY WAVED GOODBYE to the children and teachers who'd loaded onto the school bus. For their first day at the farm they'd accomplished an amazing amount of work.

When she had first approached two elementary schools with her idea, she hadn't expected immediate support. In her nine years with the Peace Corps she'd come to accept that every request got bogged down in tedious bureaucracy. So she'd gone to the initial school meeting armed with proof that programs of the type she proposed were successful in other areas, including in urban settings where kids grew flowerpot gardens.

Surprisingly she had found a dedicated staff already deeply worried about an excess of poverty-stricken families. She'd only had to mention that kids loved to eat what they grew and the principals and their staff were all in. In addition to arranging to transport third-graders out to her farm once a week, teachers at all grade levels asked if she might provide fresh vegetables for their Backpack Fridays, where they sent every child home with a backpack filled with foodstuffs. For some it was all they'd have to eat over the weekend.

Of course she'd agreed. But the meeting had opened her eyes to how many families in her area were in need. She hadn't expected to hear that US families ever went without food. In truth, she'd like to give away everything she raised, but that wasn't possible. She needed to sell enough to make ends meet and to pay her workers. She was still dipping into her savings and her dad's insurance.

The bus stopped at the end of the lane, waiting for the automatic gate to open. After it drove out Molly watched the gate close again. She stood there thinking back to the other day when the man from some oil company had parked on the main road and hiked onto her land.

A closed gate couldn't keep somebody out if they really wanted to get in.

She shivered.

Henry was probably right in saying the whole perimeter should be fenced. But fencing was costly. And what about the land sloping to the river? She irrigated from there. Yes she had seen people cross the river who shouldn't. Her dad's philosophy and that of her grandfather's had been to live and let live. She did the same.

Now that the children were gone, she unhooked Nitro's leash. He never roamed far from her side, but he liked being free to sniff out a rabbit or two.

"Come on, boy. I need to go to the barn to look at the latest application." The man who'd ridden in on the motorcycle.

As she made her way to the office Molly wasn't sure she should hire Adam Hollister, even if he ticked all the boxes. Something about him had thrown her off balance. It went beyond how easily he'd won over her dog—her supposed guard dog.

Revisiting the impression the man had left brought him squarely back into focus.

At thirty-two she could count on one hand the men who'd stirred her. A fellow Ag student in college. He'd changed his major to computers, eloped with his high school sweetheart and gone on to make his mark at IBM.

The other had been a doctor volunteering in Kenya while he did advanced studies on jungle fevers. She'd thought they'd had a future until a female physician had showed up to work as part of Molly's extended team. Mark Lane, MD, had broken her heart when he and Penelope Volker, having snagged twin fellowships at Johns Hopkins, had left without even a backward glance.

Worse, the couple's dual departure had left only a nurse and a nurse practitioner to care for the desperately ill who showed up at their village Peace Corps compound.

Shaking off the memory, she entered the barn and strained to see in the dim light. Nitro loped over to drink water from a big bowl they kept filled for him.

Henry stepped out from the office. "Molly, I think we've found you a truck driver. I checked his references and the folks he listed all said you'd be lucky to get him."

"Really?"

He handed her the double-sided application she'd put together after placing the ad.

"Where has he worked before? Why isn't he working there now? Or, if he is, why is he looking to change jobs?"

"He's currently working at a bar near Catarina. For a friend. The guy said Hollister has done everything from ordering to serving to cleaning up to being his bouncer in just short of two years. He pretty much ran the place, because the owner was renovating a house. Oh, and he also said when the bar was closed Hollister picked up housing materials and helped with construction."

"Hmm." Molly glanced over the form. On the line about education he'd written "some college."

"His second reference, Kevin Cole, has a Dallas address and phone number. Did Hollister work in Dallas?"

"That's Cole's private cell number. He said Hollister handled a lot of different projects. I asked if he could drive a diesel truck.

Cole laughed and said Hollister never met a job he couldn't handle. I gathered he lived in Dallas but worked in different places—even doing contract jobs overseas. Cole was vague. I figured it must've been for the government. Government guys are hard to pin down."

Molly chewed on that. Even working in remote Africa she'd met some black ops guys. Tough men. Shadowy figures. From her brief assessment of Adam Hollister, he fit the image.

Did she want someone like him on her payroll? Perhaps she should do more of a background check.

On the other hand, she needed someone now. It was worth giving him a trial, she supposed.

"You can always fire him if he doesn't work out," Henry said, making Molly wonder if her thoughts were that transparent.

"I can, but you know I'm better at hiring than firing."

Her cell phone rang, cutting off Henry's remark. Dragging it out of her pocket, Molly saw the call was from Tess Warner, an artisan bread maker she'd met at a farmers' market near Cotulla.

"Hey," Molly said as she answered, gesturing to Henry that the call was going to take a while. "I haven't seen you out and about at any markets for a while. Is everything okay?"

"Great!" Tess replied. "Has it really been that long?"

"A few weeks at least. Where've you been?"

"Corpus, if that counts as going anywhere." She laughed. "I guess we haven't seen each other since I tracked down an old friend of my grandmother's. The woman still lives in Sicily.

"Gabriella sent me a bunch of recipes in Italian. I needed my mom and my aunts to translate them, so I've been in Corpus trying out the recipes and transcribing them into English."

"I miss you! I toasted my last slice of your cranberry-pecan bread this morning for breakfast."

"Funny, I have loaves waiting to bake. I called to invite you over and to ask if you could bring some fresh dill. I'm home and baking up a storm. If you come over, we'll have warm bread slathered with butter and some wine my mother made."

"How can I refuse an offer like that? I have a lot to tell you, too, Tess. My truck driver got beaten up. He's the second one—the other guy quit on me."

"That's horrible. I hope you're okay."

"I've been hauling loads to markets all week in my SUV and nobody seems to bother me."

"Just the thought is bad enough. Hey, bring Nitro. Coco misses him."

"Wait until you hear how my big scary dog totally caved over a guy I may hire as my next driver."

"A new man? Wonderful, I can't wait to hear."

Molly said goodbye and turned to leave the barn.

Henry called out, "Tomorrow we'll have a large load. A lot of buyers stock up mid-week. Do you want me to call Hollister to see if he can be here and ready to hit the road by seven?"

Frowning, Molly again scanned the application she forgot she still held.

"Do you have time to run a check at the DMV on his license?"

"Sure. You're doing too much on your own. If we hire Hollister, it'll free you up to do what you like best—dig in the dirt."

"You know me too well. Okay, if his license is current, offer him the job. Did you talk to him about salary?"

Henry plucked at his lower lip. "I don't recall him asking about money. Not usual. But he didn't strike me as a man with champagne tastes. Know what I mean?"

"Okay. Suggest the same rate I paid Ramon. If he wants more, go up fifty dollars a week. But that's tops. If he's good with that and can work tomorrow, no need to let me know. If he backs out and I have to juggle my workload again, put a note on my kitchen door. I don't know how late I'll be at Tess's. She's offering bread and wine."

"Your papa would like seeing you get out with friends your age. But he would've liked it better if you were going out with a young man."

Snorting, Molly handed back Adam Hollister's application. "Don't you be stepping into Dad's shoes and giving me a hard time. Maybe I'll choose to remain single."

The old man, who'd been like a grandfather to Molly, raised an eyebrow but ducked back into the office without saying another word.

Molly went to the house with Nitro, stopping to cut and bag stalks of dill from the herbs lining her front porch. She added rosemary and thyme to the burlap bag. That barely left time for a speedy shower.

After dressing, she worked equally fast and tossed together ingredients for a summer salad. Placing the bowl on ice in a small cooler, she pocketed dog treats and left the house with twelve minutes to reach Tess's.

The freeway made the drive easy. Still, she was a tad late. Because her windows were rolled down, she smelled the fresh bread when she turned onto her friend's street. There weren't a lot of homes nearby, but the people living closest must drool a lot, she thought. Few things set a person's taste buds tingling as did warm, fresh bread.

She parked behind Tess's car, collected everything and clipped a leash on Nitro.

Tess had already thrown open her front door, greeting Molly with a hug as she crested the top step. Her friend's chubby three-year-old beagle barked and dashed out to rub noses with the much taller Doberman, who acted silly again, the way he had with Adam Hollister. The big dog scooched toward Coco on his belly, uttering what could only be described as crooning. "You ham," she accused him as she and Tess laughed.

"I thought my last batch of bread would be out of the kiln out back before you got here," Tess said. "I'll pour us each a glass of Mom's sangria and we can let the dogs run in the backyard while we wait. It feels like ages since we even talked."

"It all sounds heavenly. I've scarcely sat down all day." Molly handed Tess the burlap bag of herbs and followed her through the dimly lit living room into the bright, cheery kitchen. Molly had only been here once before.

Now, as Tess poured wine, Molly opened her cooler and stored the salad in the fridge.

Then she unhooked Nitro's leash. It took about ten seconds for the dogs to dash out through the doggie door, and for Molly to wind his leash through the handles of the cooler. Straightening, she noticed the wall of floor-to-ceiling metal racks filled with cooling loaves of bread.

"You've been baking up a storm." She accepted the glass of chilled sangria from the woman who was four years her junior, six inches shorter but much curvier. "Cheers," Molly said, touching the rim of the stemware to Tess's glass.

"I'm making up for lost time. When I visited my family as long as I did, I put a dent in my bank account. Let's go outside."

Tess elbowed open the back door and the smell of baking bread wafted in on the evening breeze. A red glow flickering in the domed wood-fired oven emitted enough light to make the porch feel cozy.

Molly sat on the bench that flanked a rustic table. "How do you know the right amount of wood to make bread bake at the temperature you need?"

"Practice," Tess said, taking a sip of wine.

"Also, when I had the stove built I installed temperature gauges in the fire box and the oven. See that digital readout? The oven is basically like one my grandmother would have used in Sicily, but with modern bells and whistles." She went over to check both gauges. Returning, she sat and said, "A few more minutes and I can pull the loaves. Is that long enough to tell me who in the world beat up your truck driver and why?"

Molly heaved a sigh. "I still don't know. Ramon didn't recognize any of his assailants. The local deputy claims they have no suspects. Between us, I doubt he'd tell me if they found the culprits... Has anyone objected to how you sell your bread?"

"How so? I've got two types of ovens, which lets me operate under cottage food industry laws. Why would they object? Who objects to you selling organic vegetables? Wait, don't answer. Let me pull out the loaves first."

The dogs raced up the steps and flopped near Molly, who took two treats from her pocket and fed one to each dog.

"Where were we?" Tess asked, stepping over Coco to take her seat.

"Discussing the harassment of my drivers. I'm disheartened after talking to Deputy Powell. He insinuated that locals think I hire undocumented immigrants, or at least supply them with food. He didn't mince words when he said I should be more circumspect about which hungry families I give produce to."

"Why is that their business? It's your food. If I didn't take pre-orders, which pretty much ensure I sell out every time, I'd donate leftovers. Also, are they leaning on the big ranchers or area builders? For sure they don't check status when they hire."

Molly shrugged and dipped a slice of orange out of her glass and ate the pulp.

"What are you going to do about a driver?"

"With luck, Henry's hired a guy today who answered an ad I ran. I didn't interview him, but we spoke. He's...well, he rides a Harley, dresses like a biker and doesn't strike me as the type to take any guff."

Tess grinned.

"So, tell me. It's not my imagination that

your tone changed when you described him. I take it he's hot?"

"Don't be silly." Molly sipped her wine. "When do we eat? The smell of your cranberry bread makes me want to tear into a loaf right now."

Tess hopped up again to check. "The bread is cool enough to move. But don't think changing the subject will make me forget about your hot biker guy. I'll ply you with more of Mom's wine."

"I didn't say he was hot. And one glass is my limit. I'm driving."

"Hot was implied. I understand if you want to keep him for yourself. How old is he, out of curiosity?"

Molly jumped up and stepped over dogs to help carry in the rack. "Honestly, Tess, did I even say he's single?"

"A motorcycle jock? Of course he is." The younger woman juggled her end of the rack, walking backward into the house.

"Hey, that's judgmental! I'd say he's close to forty. At that age—if he's single—he's probably divorced. Enough about my maybe new driver. I'll get the salad. I see the table is set."

"Spoilsport." Tess sighed. "My mom bugged me about not having a man in my life while I was visiting, so it's been on my mind. She thinks twenty-eight is over the hill. Of course she was married at seventeen and had me at eighteen. And at forty-six, she's outlived three husbands. Preferred older men."

"Wow, don't tell her I'm thirty-two and still single. She'll think I'm a bad influence." Molly held up a cruet filled with oil and herbs she found in the fridge. "Is this the dressing?"

"That's a new recipe I got from Aunt Luisa. And grab the blue container, will you? I whipped some butter with fresh berries."

Molly eyed everything once it was on the table. "I wish I liked to cook. For me it's a chore," she said, sitting. "My dad hired a cook. I tracked after Dad with the cattle, in the barn, riding horses. I was too much of a tomboy to care about cooking."

"We're both products of our backgrounds. My mom has five sisters, and being a big Sicilian family, every meal is reason to gather and eat big. Everyone cooks, and bread is a staple." She tore off a chunk of warm bread and passed the loaf to Molly.

"If you hire that new driver," she asked, "will you quit going to your booths at the markets?"

"I'll still deliver on weekends. My drivers typically work five days. And, during peak season, we have high demand six or seven days a week."

"Good. Let me know what days and which markets you'll be at. I'll adjust my schedule so maybe we can grab lunch or dinner together. I didn't make friends here until I met you."

Molly nodded. "It's the same for me, even though I grew up here. Most of my high school friends have left the area. My college friends weren't from around here. They're spread all over the globe now."

"Mom says if I'd gone to college I'd be married by now. But of my former friends who went on to university, those who moved back to Corpus act like I'm a lamebrain or something."

"They're the lame ones." Molly sat back with a sigh. "You have tons of talent."

"Oh, you are good for my ego. Do you have time to watch a movie?"

"I'd love it, but unfortunately I've got to get home."

"Well, here, let me send you off with a loaf of cranberry bread at least."

"No, you won't. I'm buying one of those and a loaf of dark rye. It'll save me chasing you down at one of the markets only to find you've sold out." She pulled out her billfold.

"Shall I put you on my weekly e-newsletter?

"Please do." Molly counted out cash and set the bread aside, admiring Tess's logo on the bags: colorful hearts around the words Bread From The Heart.

"I wish I had something clever to call my business other than McNair Gardens. But Dad already had the arch that said McNair Cattle. It was simpler to change out *Cattle* for *Gardens*."

Taking her cup to the dishwasher, she said, "We'll have to do this again. My house next," she said, picking up the bread she'd bought.

"Perfect. I guess if I miss anything about home, it's that my aunts, uncles and cousins were always popping in and out, bringing food and games."

Molly tickled Nitro. He got up, shook himself and yawned. Coco sprang up and wagged her tail. "The few times we've talked I've never thought to ask if you have siblings."

"No. My mom picked older husbands who didn't want kids of their own. And she was honest about saying her big family lacked money to go around. She wanted better for me. My dad died when I was five. Luckily I had cousins who were like siblings."

"I used to wish my dad would remarry and have kids so I'd have siblings," Molly mused. "Dad claimed he was a one-woman man. People said that was noble. Now that I'm older I think it was an excuse to not risk being hurt again. Cowardly, even."

"Maybe not. None of us can really know why another person makes the choices they make."

"I guess I feel so alone in the world since he died. My mom was orphaned and grew up in foster care. Dad's family all died before him."

Tess put a hand out and squeezed Molly's arm. "I'll be your pretend sister. Truly, if anything says we need to get away from our work and mingle more, you just reminded us that we're both such loners."

"Did I sound totally pathetic? All this talk of family made me melancholy." Striving to regain her earlier joy, Molly hugged Tess and headed for her SUV. The dogs both whined.

Tess captured Coco and they stood on the porch until Molly backed out onto the street.

Nitro hunkered down in the backseat.

It wasn't that late. But traffic on the freeway seemed extra light. Normally this section was heavily traveled by trucks crossing the border at Nuevo Laredo, although her dad had thought more traffic crossed south at Reynosa, which lead into McAllen. Molly sometimes sold produce in small towns inland from Laredo. But the lion's share of her business was north of the ranch, toward San Antonio.

It was dark by the time she exited the freeway onto the two-lane road angling toward the ranch. A crescent moon brought out the glitter of stars high overhead. Molly recalled how she used to like riding herd with her father at night.

African nights in the village were even darker, and the stars bigger, closer, for lack of any outdoor lighting.

A rare shooting star caused Molly to brake. She looked for others, but when there weren't any more, she took the one as a good omen.

Her SUV bumped for a short distance along the private lane that cut across McNair land to the archway entrance. An automatic eye registered her vehicle and she let the engine idle while waiting for the big gate to swing open. Where, as a girl, sagebrush had lined the route from here to the house, now carefully tended vegetable fields flashed green in the arc of her headlights.

As if sensing where they were, Nitro sat up, stuck his head over the seat and panted in Molly's ear. She reached back and rubbed his nose. "Almost home, boy. Tonight was fun, wasn't it?"

All at once she saw a slight movement off to her left near the path that ran between bush and pole beans. Her SUV hit a pronounced dip in the road and by the time she'd climbed out onto level ground again, whatever she'd seen was gone.

Nitro began growling and sprang against the right back window.

"Easy, boy. I don't see anything now."

Instead of driving head-on into the carport, she turned around and backed in, which left her high beams illuminating the field. Her dad had always carried a loaded handgun beneath his front seat, and often had a rifle prominently displayed in a back window gun rack. Molly had lost count of the number of times he'd counseled her to do the same since she'd come back to nurse him through the cancer.

She knew how to shoot. He'd taught her well. But she didn't like handling guns and believed they could be turned against a hesitant owner.

Nitro continued to paw at the window even after she shut off the motor and let the lights die. She could turn him loose to investigate, but didn't, because the shadow might be a coyote. Instead, she clipped on his leash, collected her bread, left the cooler and ran up the three steps to her front door with her key out. She quickly unlocked it and turned on a hall light and the one on the porch.

It was plain by his frenzied barking that Nitro's keen senses had picked up a scent.

Locking the door, she dragged Nitro into the kitchen and snapped on the bright overheads. Her heart racing, she unleashed Nitro and quickly turned out the kitchen light again. Silencing the dog with a treat, she eased over to the window and scanned the area where she'd seen—something.

Nothing moved. Not even a leaf.

Nitro padded over to his water bowl and proceeded to lap at it noisily.

Still, it took time for Molly's nerves to settle. Not normally easily frightened, she chalked it up to the attack on her two truck drivers followed by the veiled warnings from the deputy and the less-veiled caution from her insurance agent. He, of course, probably felt compelled to act in her father's stead as they'd been lifelong friends.

Belatedly she remembered asking Henry to stick a note on her front door if he wasn't able to hire the new driver so she could prepare to go to market again herself. Eventually, convinced she'd let herself be spooked over something that meant her no harm— even if a poor, hungry person had been trying to steal green beans—she opened the kitchen door and checked all around for a note. Finding none, she closed it with a sigh of relief. For now one problem had been solved. She had a driver.

Setting her alarm for 5:00 a.m., she spent a moment drawing a rough map of Adam Hollister's first-day route.

Since one person couldn't sell at all farmers' markets at once, she had local moms manage her booths. The women kept careful records and never cheated her out of a dime. She trusted them more than, say, for instance, men who ran oil companies.

Which reminded Molly she hadn't looked

up the company listed on the card that rep had given her. Maybe tomorrow. Now she was too tired.

IN THE MORNING, right after breakfast, Molly walked out to the spot where last night she'd seen an unclear motion. The area hadn't been irrigated so the path had no distinct footprints. She didn't see any sign to indicate someone had tried to pick in the dark. Peering down into the rows of the pole beans, she thought dirt may have been disturbed in a few places. Coyotes wouldn't dig. They chased mice and squirrels. But if a migrant happened to be traveling with a dog…

She met the first crew of pickers and directed them to the fields with the produce slated to be sold later that morning in a series of small towns that fell in a circle. The eastern sky banded with faint streaks of gold, and Molly's crew had just fanned out to pick when she heard the rumbling of a motorcycle. Shading her eyes, she watched her new driver stop next to the silo. Glancing at her watch, she noted that he had showed up about two hours earlier than she'd expected him.

Nitro left his favorite spot under the pecan tree and made a beeline for the newcomer. Molly ground her back teeth together. What was it about Hollister, she wondered, watching her guard dog act like a puppy chasing his tail?

She stepped nearer, at once noticing the man's broad grin as he removed his helmet. She took in the wrinkles around his eyes, which yesterday she'd termed stormy but altered her perception today. He seemed more approachable.

"You're early," she said.

He straightened, still smiling. "Henry said I'd need to fill out tax withholding forms. He suggested I might tour the farm to get an idea of what's planted where."

"Oh, sure." Taking off her gloves, Molly tucked them under her belt. She grew warm feeling the man's gaze follow her movement. She wore a faded red tank top and jeans with a ripped knee.

Today he was wearing a moss-green,

long-sleeved, snap-buttoned shirt and jeans a few washings newer than hers.

Striding past him, she twirled a dial lock and started to open one of the double barn doors. Feeling suddenly surrounded by bulky warmth, Molly froze and glanced back, only to find Adam reaching around her to help.

"Sorry, I didn't mean to startle you," he said. "That door looks heavy. I thought I'd give you a hand. Do you want it all the way open?"

"Uh, fine." She let go and ducked out from under his solid arm. "Henry generally has them wide open. The office is there. Well, you'd know that from filling out the application—" she said, breaking off with a shrug. "I'll get the W-4 forms and a map of how the gardens are laid out." She stopped again, feeling as if she was running off at the mouth.

"Would you have time to give me the fifty-cent tour?"

It wasn't a task she'd choose, but since he hadn't listed farming on his application form, it said something that he was eager to see what she grew.

"I'll show you around the upper fields planted with produce you'll be hauling to market this week. My land slopes a mile down to within fifty feet of the river. I have a few hundred acres stretching into McMullen County. The lower part is planted in cabbage and some cranberries. The adjacent section lies fallow now. I hope to add nut trees and citrus soon."

He finished filling out the two forms she'd handed him, and looked up in surprise. "I didn't realize you owned so much land."

"My dad ran cattle until he got too sick. Some say my plan to plant it all so it produces year-round is too ambitious."

"Hmm." Adam cleared his throat. "Does your husband do the plowing, harrowing and irrigating? You know...the heavy work."

Molly set his forms on Henry's desk and scowled. "I'm single. This is all my baili-wick. I have degrees in agriculture and organic farming. Come on, we'll start your tour."

Inclining his head, Adam fell in behind her.

"I'm impressed," he said some half hour later when they ended up at the truck he'd be driving.

She reached inside the cab and removed a ring with several pages attached. Flipping a few, she selected one. "My crates are color-coded. This sheet shows the code and your stops for today. It lists addresses for the open-air markets. My booths have signs that read McNair Gardens. Your contact is listed above each address." She turned the page. "This tells which colored crates you leave at which market. You'll offload those, pick up empties and a money bag with the previous day's receipts."

He took the binder, but pinned her with a serious look. "Henry said you'd be accompanying me today and tomorrow."

"What? No. Why? He didn't leave a note telling me that."

"He said Spanish is the primary language of your sales staff. To say mine is rusty would be stretching my abilities. He also said they may hesitate to trust me because your last driver had some problems."

"My booth handlers are all studying English if they aren't already fluent."

But other things ran through Molly's mind. For one, she pictured running into Tess, to whom she'd vehemently denied that Adam was hot. Today he totally fit the description.

After waging a fierce internal debate she conceded Henry had a point about her staff's anxiety. "All right. Here's the ignition key." She dug the fob out of her pocket. "Drive down to the lower road. Park between the tomatoes and kale and we'll load up."

CHAPTER THREE

"I DIDN'T SEE any kids working in your fields today," Adam later said casually, trying to hide that he was relieved. Seeing them had been like plunging a knife in his heart. Until then he hadn't realized how he'd painstakingly avoided going places where he might run into moms and their kids.

"They'll be back Thursdays until their planting is ready to harvest. I sprouted their seeds in my greenhouse so they won't have to wait so long to see results. Hopefully the plants they set out will all be edible before school ends."

"I don't get it. Are you teaching a class in gardening or is it a class kids take in school?"

The two of them were moving crates from the ends of rows where pickers had steadily filled them. Molly carried crates to the truck and Adam lifted them onto the flatbed in the order she dictated—the order on the chart she'd given him.

"It's not a formal class," she said, and jumped up onto the truck to arrange the crates. "I consider it a hands-on learning experience that leads to good eating habits. Kids gain an appreciation for healthy foods because they like to eat what they help grow. Don't you agree?"

Adam sort of bobbed his head as he stacked two crates of tomatoes in the spot where she pointed. "I'm impressed by how you have all of this committed to memory. I'm sorry, but you're getting ahead of me."

Molly smiled. "If you stick around long enough, remembering which color crate goes to which market becomes a habit."

"You mean markets receive the same color crate on set days even if the contents change? Today we have lettuce, tomatoes, peas, carrots and radishes. But in looking over your fields, the harvest will change. I notice your corn has good-size ears."

"Right. See, you're getting the hang of my process already, and you didn't start out working with the earth like my previous two drivers."

"Do you mind if I ask why they left?" Pausing, Adam leaned on a stack of crates and gazed up at Molly.

"I would've thought Henry had told you." Molly sighed. "Last fall my first driver claimed he was hassled by some men he said followed him to a market and shoved him around. He was known to complain a lot, so I ignored him. He quit and left the area." She frowned. "My second driver's reliable. He used to work cattle for my dad. A couple of weeks ago he was run off the road and beaten up. Maybe by the same men. They frightened him into quitting driving. He still works for me, but behind the scenes. Listen, I'll understand if you don't want the job. I can rerun the ad."

"Are you trying to get rid of me?"

Looking down on him, standing tall and loose-limbed, wearing a crooked little smile, Molly debated with herself about how to answer. She settled on muttering, "No, no, of course not. I hate driving the truck in freeway traffic. During my time with the Peace

Corps I only drove a beat-up Jeep on what would be considered here as cow paths. Pass me more crates, please. Markets open before the sun gets too high."

"Sure." Adam quickly set half a dozen full crates at her feet. "So you served in the Peace Corps?"

"Mmm-hmm." She gave a noncommittal shrug.

He jogged past the truck to other rows and returned with more crates of ripe tomatoes. "Getting back to your former drivers. What do you think they did to make enemies?"

"Funny, the sheriff I spoke to seemed to think the enemies are mine."

"Really?" Adam shaded his eyes and gave her a thorough once-over. "You don't strike me as someone who'd irritate men."

His close scrutiny sent a hot flush to Molly's cheeks. Recovering, she shot back, "Don't count on that. May I ask what gives you such insight into how someone makes enemies? Might it correlate to jobs you did for Mr. Cole?"

Adam fumbled and almost dropped the

crate he'd picked up. "Uh, you talked to Kevin?"

"Henry did."

"What did Kev have to say? I haven't seen him in a while. I only spoke to his secretary."

Molly tossed her head. "Henry said he was vague. He guessed you handled some kind of government job. Mr. Cole told Henry you did some work out of the country. Were you a mercenary?" she asked abruptly.

Adam laughed. "Nothing so exciting. Try engineering." He dropped three crates at her feet and left to retrieve a new batch.

"Oh." It wasn't until he glanced back over one wide shoulder, his eyes curious, that Molly realized she may have sounded disappointed.

And maybe she was.

The rough-and-tumble life she'd made up for him meant he could handle whatever guys wanted to disrupt her business. Also, soldier of fortune fit him. At least it fit his looks.

Adam squinted up at her again. "I have another question. Since you send certain produce to specific markets each day, do buyers always go there looking for those foods? I'm trying to understand this business."

"Dedicated shoppers may travel to more than one market a week. Is that what you mean?"

"Yeah, but what does your sales staff do, say, if more people show up in a morning than they can accommodate? Are there food fights? I'm thinking of a tool sale I attended once where guys came to blows over a limited number of drills."

She laughed. "Food fights? Farmers' markets...aren't like that. Have you never been to one?" When he shook his head, she took a deep breath and explained. "Regulars know to go early. They buy what's available. Occasionally we have a few vegetables left over. People who can't afford to buy wander back at the end of the day to see if vendors have produce to give away."

Adam straightened. "Is that a racket? I mean, couldn't someone who can afford to buy food game the system?"

"Why would they? People are proud. No one *wants* a handout."

He might have made another remark, but Henry drove up, parked and climbed from his aged pickup.

She still had questions about Adam. For instance, he'd said he'd been an engineer for Mr. Cole, but on his application under education, he'd written "some college." The engineers she'd met in the Peace Corps had had a lot of years of university and bragged about it. So had this man quit college?

Nitro jumped up from his shady spot between the bean rows. He remained on alert until he recognized Henry, then he sank down again in the cool dirt.

"Good morning, you two. Glad to see you showed up early, Adam." The older man plucked a couple of pea pods out of a crate and ate the peas. Dropping the pods, he smiled. "Sweet. Way better than in the supermarkets."

Molly stopped shifting crates on the truck bed. "Why would you buy peas at the supermarket when you can walk out in the field and pick all you want?"

"Shouldn't we check out the competition? Just kidding. I tagged along while Alma did our grocery shopping last night. You aren't charging enough for peas or string beans."

Henry and Molly discussed pricing while Adam collected more crates he then set at Molly's feet.

Henry turned his attention back to Adam. "You wearing a back support belt?"

Molly paused in lashing down a row to stare at the man who'd just shed his long-sleeved shirt. A white undershirt molded to bands of rippling muscles, making Henry's question seem silly. Adam Hollister had back muscle and every other kind of muscle to spare.

"We have back belts in the barn for the taking. I know, I know…" Henry waved a hand as if to erase Adam's anticipated objection. "At your age, I scoffed, too. Now I have a bad back. Miss Molly's daddy grumped because she never wears one."

She realized that comment brought Adam's scrutiny to her again. "I should set a good example," she said. "But they're hot."

"How much do you suppose one of these full crates weighs?" Adam asked.

"They vary." Molly scooted crates filled with eggplant into four separate lines.

Henry answered. "According to OSHA rules those cucumbers are heavy enough to do some muscle damage."

Molly made a face. "Okay, okay. Point taken. This is the last of this load. We'll stop at the barn and get back support belts, and use them when we unload. The last thing I need is a squabble with the government's Occupational Safety and Health Administration." She lashed down the last two rows of crates and jumped off the truck.

"Adam, if you'll drive up to the barn, I'll get Nitro and meet you and Henry there."

Nodding, he retrieved his shirt from a bean pole and climbed into the cab.

Henry got into his pickup and, after a sputter or two of the ancient motor, drove off.

Molly stopped to thank the pickers whose day was done. "Come to the office for your pay. Anyone who can return tomorrow will pick summer squash, carrots and radishes.

Some of you will cut romaine lettuce. If you've done lettuce, you know it goes slower since we twist Organically Grown marketing bands around each head." She repeated what she'd said in Spanish. When no one asked questions, she got Nitro and set off for the barn.

The men stood talking inside the open double doors.

"Henry, would you mind giving Adam the back belts to put in the truck? I'll open the safe and pay the workers."

"Are they finished?" Adam said in clear surprise. "They can't have earned very much in such a short day." He followed Molly to the office, but took the belts Henry handed him.

"You maybe didn't notice. They are all women. Most have school-age children at home caring for younger siblings until Mom gets back. They start here at dawn. The short work day suits them." She spun the dial on a big floor safe, opened the heavy door and took out a stack of clipboards and a money sack.

Adam disappeared with the belts. He

came straight back and watched Molly spread clipboards across a big oak desk. She opened a money bag and pulled out stacks of bills and smaller sacks of coin. Taking a seat behind the desk, she glanced past Adam and smiled at a petite woman in a worn cotton housedress. "Luisa, bring me your crate slips."

The woman made herself smaller to slip past the big man in the doorway. "Excuse me," he said, scrambling to step aside.

Molly took the woman's colored slips, counted them out and recorded numbers on pages clipped to the boards. "You picked like a whirlwind today," she said. Wasting no time, she counted out money and handed it to the woman, who tucked it in a pocket of her dress. In a soft voice she said she'd be back the next day.

One at a time the others filed in to be paid. The entire exercise took only fifteen minutes.

Leaning a shoulder against the wall, Adam asked, "Why do you pay people every day?"

"I don't pay everyone. Only the pickers.

The farm crew get checks each Friday because they make a set wage. As you will, too. I trust that works for you."

"Sure. Whatever," he said.

"Henry," Molly called. "Could you put this away and lock the safe? We need to hit the road. I'll post to the computer when we finish. Since you volunteered me to ride along with Adam, I'll collect the market receipts and do the banking. It's only a few blocks out of the way of our last stop."

Henry bustled into the office. "I figured you'd show him the ropes. I'd do it, but when I finish here I'm needed in the east pasture—sorry, old habits die hard. I mean the east garden. Rick phoned. Someone stole our irrigation heads."

Molly stopped short of the door.

"Good thing you bought extra when you upgraded the filtration system," Henry added. "I'll take him new ones and help install them. I think we need to get water on the onions."

"Who on earth would steal irrigation heads?" she asked.

Henry shrugged as he stacked her paperwork back in the safe. "Dunno. Maybe migrants who think they're worth selling for junk."

"Are they copper?" Adam asked. He'd moved into the conversation and now stood directly behind Molly. "It's been all over the news lately that thieves are stripping every possible shred of copper wire and fixtures. Apparently that's a lucrative black market."

"I think our fixtures are brass," Molly said, her brow furrowed. "Do we even have a dozen new heads, Henry?"

"I checked. We have exactly twelve. I'll pull the paperwork so you can reorder. With the weather turning warmer, you'll lose crops aplenty without regular irrigation."

Molly's frown deepened. "Who would steal sprinkler heads?"

"You already asked that." Adam shifted his gaze from Henry to her.

"Yes, and I may ask it again. Let's go." She whistled for Nitro and he bounded out of the shadowy barn.

Lengthening her stride, she reached the truck before Adam, and she had the passenger door open with the dog inside by the time she felt his big hands close around her waist. She jerked away in shock. "What are you doing?"

His expression turned puzzled. "Helping you into the cab."

"I'm capable of climbing into a truck. Get in your own seat and start this beast." She tried to prove her agility, but her right boot slipped off the high step. Had Adam not still been in a position to steady her, she probably would have fallen on her backside.

To the man's credit, he didn't say a word. He gave her a boost and put his sunglasses on as he rounded the white cab of the Ford F-650.

"Uh, thanks," she muttered. "That's what comes from being too cocky," she added, nudging Nitro over so she had room to sit and buckle in. Still, she glanced at Adam out of the corner of her eye. He seemed fully engaged with starting the truck, shifting it into gear and driving toward the gate.

Point in his favor. No matter that she'd like to think, under similar circumstances, likely she would've rubbed it in. Or laughed at least.

He pulled out a cell phone, set it where he could see it on the dash, and tapped it a few times. "I took the liberty of loading the market addresses into my GPS."

Downshifting, Adam passed through the gate and pulled onto the county road.

"Ramon always ground the gears. Have you driven commercial big rigs?"

Adam spared her a glance that fell away when Nitro flopped down and used his thigh as a head pillow.

"I'll move him if he's bothering you," Molly said. "It's really odd. We took classes so he'd be my guard dog. He growled at Henry for months. Yet you're his instant buddy."

"I haven't got an explanation. I haven't had a dog since I was a kid. But he doesn't bother me. And to answer your previous question, I've driven more kinds of vehicles than I can name, including some with the steering wheel on the right."

Molly studied him. "You didn't give me any references from abroad. I assume the company you worked for was based in Dallas."

"Yes." Slowing, Adam swung onto the freeway on-ramp.

"According to Henry, your boss in Dallas was light on specifics. His guess was that you did government work."

His eyes on the side-view mirror as he merged with traffic, Adam mumbled, "Some. Yeah."

"Sounds like that job would be way more exciting than bartending in rural Texas. Why did you leave?"

Silence stretched between them for several seconds. Long enough for Molly to look directly at him and see his jaw tighten and throat muscles working. She thought he wasn't going to answer.

"I left Dallas for personal reasons," he said with a ragged edge to his voice. As if to put a defined period at that end of his statement, he stabbed a finger at his phone. "My GPS indicates I should exit at the next ramp. What's the procedure at the first market?"

"Oh, uh…" Molly felt she'd crossed some line she hadn't meant to. Quickly she gathered herself. "There's a road of sorts that runs behind the stalls. Vendor vehicles enter at the north end. You can stop behind our booth. Pull up as close as possible to give other trucks room to pass. Listen, I'm sorry. I didn't mean to hit a nerve."

This time he didn't remark but concentrated on driving, navigating the poorly marked streets that led to the outdoor market.

By then the sun had burned through the morning smog that hung over Laredo. Molly directed Adam down an alley and told him where to stop.

Her two helpers were already at the booth. "Eva, Inarosa, meet Adam, my new driver."

He left off unhooking bungee cords and touched two fingers to his head by way of a greeting. The women knew Ramon had quit. Still, they gaped at him a moment, said, *"¡Hola!"* in unison and took the crates he handed down.

"Adam doesn't speak much Spanish," Molly told them. "Be patient. Look at it as a great chance to practice your English." The pair nodded. Then, because people had begun to gather at the booth, they worked to unload, and Eva went to help customers.

Adam loaded the empty crates stacked at the back of the booth without being told. Inarosa handed Molly the bank bag. She exchanged it for an empty one and they were ready to head to the next market.

"That's a well-oiled operation," Adam said. "It puts me in mind of—" He broke off and checked his phone GPS. Clearing his throat, plainly he changed what he'd started to say. "I assumed everyone shopped in grocery stores like me."

Molly wondered what he'd held back. He was obviously a man who kept his private life and thoughts close. She could respect that. Even as it made her more curious about his past. When someone claimed to have left a job and a city for personal reasons, it smacked of something like a bad romance. Or was that a woman thing? Maybe men weren't so sentimental or vulnerable. Men were more likely to pack up and leave over a disagreement with a boss. Except Adam had given his old boss as a reference. And Henry had said the guy had given Adam a glowing one.

Deep in thought, she missed his next

comment until he poked her arm. "I asked if my GPS is correct. Is our next stop Laredo?"

"Sorry. We're going into the heart of the city. This market caters to foot traffic. Border day-crossers. Have you been to Old Town? A lot of pushcart vendors operate on both sides of the Rio Grande."

When Adam shook his head, she pointed out glimpses of the river.

He braked to a crawl because the narrow street had become congested with people on three-wheeled bicycle carts.

"Some of those riders will be our customers. Most of them fill their carts and pedal over to Nuevo Laredo where they resell the food for a profit."

"Does it bother you? I mean, if you know you could drive over there and make more money yourself?"

"It's not worth it to me to have to deal with customs. They need to scrutinize every crate going and coming. My lettuce could wilt in the time it'd take to wend my way through border officials."

"Gotcha. Oh, I see the market. It's a lot more colorful than the last one."

"This market doesn't cater to the American trade. Stop right in front of our booth and let's unload as fast as we can to keep from getting ticketed for holding up traffic."

Adam parked in front of the stall Molly pointed to. It resembled a small circus tent. A red banner, stretched between the posts, read Fresco Producer in yellow.

Molly let Nitro out and made short work of introductions than at the last site. The younger of the two women set out a bowl of water for the dog. He nosed around inside the booth and found a meat bone.

"Marisol, you spoil him." Laughing, Molly paused in handling crates to hug the dark-haired, dark-eyed woman.

Luz, though, teased Molly about hanging on to her *hermoso* new driver. She seemed freer with her jokes once she learned Adam didn't speak much Spanish.

Feeling her cheeks burn, Molly rolled her eyes at the laughing women. She collected the receipt bag and hoped Adam was too busy to hear what was said. Anyone who knew a few words of Spanish could figure out Luz had pronounced him a handsome catch. Fortunately, he acted oblivious.

"Phew, this place is crazy," Adam exclaimed as he inched the truck to the end of the street.

"I love Old Town. It's teeming with color and life. The old and the new in this part of town blend really well. It's something I imagined would work in African villages," she mused. "The difference here is that big chain stores recognize they can make a profit and invest. People in rural Africa are so poor investors won't risk capital."

Adam listened attentively but she noticed he didn't venture his thoughts, so she was surprised when he eventually said, "So, your Peace Corps work was partly in Africa?"

Molly nodded. "All nine years," she admitted. "I'd still be there if not for my father being diagnosed with prostate cancer that he did nothing about until it got too bad to treat." She smudged away a tear.

"I didn't mean to upset you."

She shrugged and they were silent for a moment.

"Dad raised me," she finally said. "My mom died when I was a toddler. I wanted to think he'd live forever."

Adam faced the front, gripped the steering wheel and then, one at a time wiped his hands down his thighs. "Uh. So our last stop of the day is still in Laredo?"

"Yes, but on the way out of town. You'll see the next market serves a very different clientele. Instead of the colorful tiered skirts Luz and her daughter wear, my next managers wear jeans and T-shirts like what I have on." She grimaced and wished she hadn't brought his inspection back to her. His eyes had a way of not missing any flaw, and she had her share. "Be careful what you say around them," she warned him. "These women understand English, but aren't above pretending they don't so people gossip in front of them."

"No problem."

The process of pulling in beside the stall and unloading full crates and collecting empty ones went smoothly. Molly was pleased that Adam had gotten the hang of it.

In the cab again, she emptied all three cash bags into a cash box she pulled out from under the seat.

"Just give me the directions to the bank," he said.

She did, all the while deftly separating bills and coin.

"How are you able to count cash so fast?" Adam asked after she wrote out a deposit slip tucked in the lid and put everything in a deposit bag. "I hated closing out the bar till. I felt all thumbs."

"If I make a mistake the bank will correct it. There. The bank is on the corner. There's parking in the rear. I won't be but a few minutes."

"Good. It's lunchtime," he said, glancing at his watch. "How about if I buy you lunch somewhere, and you can help me program tomorrow's market stops into my phone?"

Molly hadn't thought about lunch. She certainly didn't want an employee to buy hers. "Sure. There's a good burger place up the road a ways. It'll be my treat. Ramon packed his lunch. Of course, he did other jobs around the farm once he finished a run."

"I can do that, too. Henry didn't mention it. But I didn't realize the driving job only took half a day."

"As early as you started, we can call it a full day this time."

"I don't want to shortchange you," he said, taking up two parking spots with the big truck. "We can negotiate over hamburgers."

"Okay." Hiking the short distance to the bank, Molly couldn't fathom what about Hollister knocked her off-kilter. He was good-looking. And big. But he didn't throw his weight around. It had to be those eyes, she decided, walking up to a teller she knew. Adam had eyes that speared right through you.

Once the deposit was done and she'd taken out enough cash to buy lunch—because she hadn't left the house with money—she dashed out to the truck. Taking her seat and buckling in, she rattled off directions.

When they reached the outskirts of town

Adam peered out his side window and drawled, "Hel…lo. We have a tail."

"A what?"

"A black Suburban with smoked windows. I noticed it trailing us when we left the last market. I thought I imagined he was following us, because he disappeared when we stopped at the bank."

Molly leaned across Nitro and strained to see what Adam was talking about. "That sounds like the vehicle Ramon said forced him off the road."

Adam stepped on the gas.

"We have to go up a steep on-ramp! There's a drop-off to the right. And no guardrail. If we were coming down, there'd only be a ditch."

"Grab hold of Nitro and brace yourself," Adam ordered.

"What are you going to do?"

"They've got a powerful engine, but we're bigger. I think we can outrun them."

"Oh." He sped up the ramp and Molly wrapped her arms around the dog. She heard a sickening scrape of metal on metal and felt the truck lurch to the right. It seemed impossible to believe, but the SUV must've hit them! Fearing they'd be forced over the side, she closed her eyes.

Sensing a subtle shift left again, Molly hauled in a deep breath. She opened her eyes when Adam quickly double-clutched and thrust the Ford into a lower gear. She jerked forward, then back. It was clear the SUV racing alongside intended to ram them again.

But when Adam hit the gas hard, as if in slow motion the black vehicle swerved sharply, crossed the median to the left and spun out.

Unable to breathe, Molly thought the SUV would flip. For a heartbeat or more, as the black vehicle plowed into the ditch, a rooster tail of dust shot up to engulf it from sight. Once the air behind them cleared, she could see it sitting sideways in the ditch.

Adam upshifted again and it took the Ford a moment to respond and begin climbing the ramp to the highway above.

Molly pressed her forehead to the back window and strained to see behind them.

"Thank heavens they didn't roll. Looks like they might have blown a tire."

"Do you want me to stop?"

She raked sweaty palms down Nitro's back. "They tried to run us off the ramp. We could be outnumbered. Or they may have guns. I'll phone Deputy Powell." Molly dug out her cell. "The burger bar is just up the road," she told Adam as she waited for her call to connect. "Powell can meet us there. I don't want to be accused of fleeing the scene of an accident that wasn't our fault."

"Any idea who they are?" Adam asked after she finished speaking to a dispatcher.

"No. I told the deputy I have no enemies. Apparently I was wrong."

CHAPTER FOUR

MOLLY TUCKED HER phone away. "Dispatch said Deputy Powell is out on a call. They promised to pass on my message. He'll check it out as soon as he can."

"It sounded like they thought the accident might not be in their jurisdiction." Adam made it a question.

"Right. I think it is, though, since it happened near the freeway. That's well outside the city limits. The dispatcher asked if we were still at the accident scene." Molly slanted Adam a worried look. "Should we have stopped? What if they say we ran them off the road?"

"Their paint is on this truck, I'm sure. Of course, maybe it's somebody who hates vegetables because their moms made them eat them as kids."

Molly didn't laugh. "I wish I knew what

their problem is. Oh, look, there's the hamburger shack just ahead on our right."

Adam pulled into a gravel parking strip. "Shack is right. Who would think a place like this would be so busy?"

"There are no other places to eat on this stretch of highway. This place has been here for years. It's family owned. Cattlemen love it because their burgers are all grade A beef. And wait until you see how big the patties are."

They ordered burger combos and a plain patty for Nitro and then had a brief tug-of-war when it came time to collect their sodas and pay the bill. Since a line had formed behind them and the woman at the cash register looked harried, each ended up paying for their own order. Adam chose a table set beneath one of many shade trees. Molly left her drink and went back to the truck for Nitro. She hooked his leash on an empty chair leg and moved it away from other tables with his water bowl from the truck.

"Is it hard to always travel with a dog?"

"No harder than for folks who travel with kids."

Adam had no comeback, and Molly again wondered if he was single at his age because he disliked kids.

Looking up at him, she noticed he was eyeing a couple with a boy and girl of around five or six who could have been twins. The family noisily claimed a table next to her and Adam.

Molly made small talk with the kids while their folks went to order. One of the first things she told them was that Nitro was a guard dog, so they shouldn't pet him.

Adam clammed up. She toyed with the idea of asking him if he was bothered by kids. But someone at the window called out their order number and he jumped up to get the tray.

By the time she'd fed Nitro, Adam—now sitting with his back to the young family—had tucked into his burger.

"Uh-oh, there's Deputy Powell." Molly set her burger back in its box and wiped her mouth and fingers on her napkin.

Adam stopped dragging a steak fry through ketchup. Then he nonchalantly ate it and was still chewing when the lawman sauntered up, propped his shiny black knee-high boot on the empty chair next to Molly, and slowly removed his aviator sunglasses.

"Well, Ms. McNair, I thought that was your farm truck." The man set his glasses and an electronic tablet on the table. "Might you have relayed bad information to our dispatcher? I drove out to where you claim an assailant tried to force you off the freeway ramp but instead landed in the opposite ditch. I saw no sign of a wreck."

Molly, who still gripped her wadded napkin, gaped at the deputy. "It happened on the ramp at milepost 107." She looked at Adam. "We should've taken down the license plate—and taken a picture on my cell. As it is," she continued to the deputy, "I didn't get a great look as we were picking up speed to climb the ramp. It was a black SUV. A late-model Chevy Suburban. I thought they blew a tire, or maybe broke an axel. I could be wrong. It was a terrifying few minutes where we were in danger of going over the embankment."

"'We'?" Deputy Powell seemed only then to notice Adam sitting adjacent to her.

"Yes, my new driver, Adam Hollister. The vehicle that rammed us fits one described by Danny and Ramon, my former drivers. They both came out on the short end of encounters with two guys in a black SUV. But I reported that."

Powell said nothing. He zeroed in on Adam, who continued to eat his lunch. "Let's have a look at your driver's license, fella."

Slowly wiping off his fingers, Adam glanced up. "Mine? Why?"

Powell hitched up his belt and extended his hand. Nitro got up and growled low in his throat, but sank down when Molly gave him a hand command.

The deputy didn't budge and he didn't seem to care that other people had stopped eating to watch. "Ms. McNair has a habit of hiring losers. If you've nothing to hide, you won't mind my running your license through DMV."

Adam stood. "Finish your meal," he told Molly. "I'll give the deputy my license and show him where the SUV left their paint on the truck's running board." Not rushing,

Adam took time to toss his empty container in the trash can. Drinking the last of his soda, he threw the cup away, as well. Only then did he walk toward the truck, never glancing back to see if the deputy was following him.

Powell took a moment to gather himself. "Where did you find him?" he asked Molly. "If he's not six feet of trouble, I don't know what is."

Molly leaned back to peer around Powell. "If I ventured a guess I'd say he's closer to six-two or three." And every inch was intriguing, she thought as she watched Adam's lazy walk. She calmly picked up her burger again.

Deputy Powell stomped away like a man on a mission. Molly trusted Adam's license was in order, because Henry had already checked it out with the Department of Motor Vehicles.

Swallowing, she wondered why local police considered her persona non grata. They'd had no qualms about hobnobbing with her dad. She remembered half a dozen officers or so attending a yearly after-roundup barbecue her father and his wranglers always held. Of course an invitation printed in the weekly newspaper opened the event up to everyone in the county.

Taking yet another bite from her now cold burger, Molly furtively studied the men inspecting the damage to her truck. She threw what remained of her meal in the trash before collecting Nitro. She shouldn't leave her newest employee to handle a problem that was hers to deal with. Although, surprisingly, Adam and Deputy Powell seemed to be gesturing congenially.

Before she reached the pair, she saw Powell look at what she presumed was Adam's license. The cop soon passed it back and the men continued talking even as Adam returned the item to his wallet then slid it into his back pocket.

Once she got close enough to hear them, it was another jolt to hear Powell say, "I'll send one of my men around to area auto body shops. If we find any reports of paint or body repairs on a black SUV, I'll talk with the owner myself."

"Thanks." Adam stuck out his hand and

the men shook. He saw Molly then and glanced her way. "You heard, I presume. I filled the deputy in on everything I can recall. Maybe you have something to add." He ticked off a short list.

Powell eyed her. As if he didn't like standing so close to the dog, he took a few steps to the side.

"You were the one who first noticed them behind us," she said, her gaze darting between the two men. "I already told the deputy I don't know why anyone wants to bother me. I, uh, didn't report this, but last night I came home after dark and I may have spooked a would-be intruder. I saw a shadow slip into a row of pole beans. Nitro went into a barking frenzy. At the time I figured it could be a wild animal. But this morning, one of my workers on irrigation detail notified Henry that someone had stolen our sprinkler heads."

"Henry Garcia?"

"Yes."

"I supposed he'd gone to work for another rancher after your dad passed. What does a lifelong cattleman know about farming?"

Molly settled Nitro, who had gone on alert and growled at Powell. "He and Alma are like family. I thought he'd retire, but he likes being busy, and overseeing my crew is easier on his old bones than punching cows. His words, not mine," Molly said through a smile.

Powell cleared his throat. "Henry came to this country the right way. He signed up and waited for a spot to open up. I wonder how he feels about a lot of those folks you feed. Probably one of them stole your irrigation parts to sell as scrap metal. Our calls on petty theft have risen tenfold in the past few years. We rarely find any of the heisted merchandise. It's smuggled back across the border and sold on the black market faster than it takes me to log a complaint."

It was on the tip of Molly's tongue to say, "Tell us how you really feel about immigration," but she didn't. Instead she turned to Adam. "If you're finished, we'd better go. I have a full afternoon scheduled."

"Fine by me. Deputy? Are we free to leave?"

The uniformed man pursed his lips and

acted as if he'd like to say more. Then he gave a curt bob of his head, hitched up his heavy belt again, making the handcuffs jingle, and turned on his heel.

Rather than return to his patrol vehicle, he headed for the fast-food joint.

Molly eased out the irritated breath she'd been holding. She lost no time rounding the cab to load Nitro in the passenger side and then climb in herself. She was connecting her seat belt by the time Adam took his seat.

"Does he think you employ illegal immigrants?" he asked, putting on his sunglasses as he stuck the key in the ignition. "And do you?"

"Fixated as he is on the subject, if he really thought I did, he or some of his staff would be out to my place checking everyone's work permits in a nanosecond."

Adam peered in both directions before pulling onto the highway. "It's plain he's got a bee up his backside. Maybe he needs to transfer out of this area. You know, go work in a town with a stagnant population of native…uh, original—" He broke off as Molly burst out laughing.

"You see the dichotomy? We took this land from Mexico. If one goes back further it probably belonged to indigenous tribes. We're the interlopers. A fact completely overlooked by people like Deputy Powell."

She sobered.

"But he has rules to enforce. So do I. I check green cards and pay social security. Some numbers may be fake, but if they are I can't tell. I do my best to obey the law, but I can't turn my back on hunger." She shrugged. "So be it."

"That makes you humane. And it's not up to you to plug the holes along the border."

"Exactly. Since I came home, especially after I sold dad's cattle and started the farm, border crossings have fallen off. Yet tempers are stoked by dissidents. I've heard rumors of vigilantism downriver. I haven't seen it here, unless it's in the form of those yokels driving a smoke-windowed SUV. I know I said it before, but it's worth repeating. I won't blame you if you quit this job. Although you got more cooperation out of Deputy Powell than I ever did. What accounts for your 'Kumbaya' moment?"

Adam shot her a veiled look. "What moment?"

"Well, I heard him tell you he'd have a deputy canvas local body shops to see if anyone got work done on a black SUV. When Ramon had his run-in with what I'm sure are probably the same guys, Roy Powell said they were likely the very people I feed. He suggested I sell the ranch and go back to Africa."

"I guess he couldn't refute tangible dings and paint scrapings the length of our running board."

"No." She shuddered. "Where do you suppose those guys got off to in such a short amount of time? Do you think Powell really went to the site?"

"I think he did. Until he saw the dents and paint, he thought we—you—had purposely sent him on a wild-goose chase."

"Why would I do that?"

Adam shrugged. "It's fairly evident you aren't a fan."

She snorted. "He brought that on himself. I wish you could have seen how he let Ramon sit in his office, bleeding and bruised. He wouldn't have done the same if it'd been you. Powell would have summoned an ambulance and had someone interview you at the hospital."

"Yes, because I would have demanded it."

"I did demand it for Ramon and he didn't care. He'd help you because he thinks it's your birthright. Members of my crew whose last names are Flores, Hernandez or Martinez aren't accorded the same courtesy."

"I get that, Molly. Which is one reason I won't bail on you."

"Thanks. But what might your other reasons be?" she asked abruptly.

He flashed her a cheeky smile. "Because I like Henry. And I like your dog." Adam reached over and scratched Nitro between his ears.

She rolled her eyes as the big dog wiggled and wagged his short tail.

"The way you handled driving during our earlier incident proved to me that you could hire on to drive for any short- or long-haul trucking outfit. Jobs that pay a whole lot more. Why mine?"

Molly thought he wasn't going to give her

more. He didn't comment until they reached the arch to the farm and he punched the remote control to open the gate. As he drove through and it closed, he said, "For a while I knocked around Texas living a tumbleweed existence, until my friend needed me to run his bar. That suited me then. Now his remodel is done, and I like this river delta. Drifting has lost its appeal. But if you want someone else, say so and I'll mosey on."

"Please don't," Molly said when Adam braked next to her barn. "I apologize for being nosy." She smiled. "A lot of that comes from the years I spent in remote African villages. It was rare to get visitors. Whenever we did we wrung every last tidbit of news about their lives in the outside world out of them."

Adam shut off the motor and pocketed the key. "I think Henry wants to talk to you." He pointed over her shoulder.

She spun to her side window and saw that Henry did look anxious. And another of her employees, Rick Canfield, hovered behind the older man. She clipped on Nitro's leash and slowly cracked open her door. "Henry? Is there trouble? Did you try to call me?"

"I didn't," he said. "I figured you'd show up soon. I wouldn't have left until you were here, anyway. And it's not a major problem. When I took the new sprinkler heads to Rick, we discovered whoever stole the other ones also stripped the pipe threads. He said the hardware store in Laredo should have a handheld bolt threader for around twenty bucks or so."

"We can buy one the exact size of the pipe," Rick said. "They aren't as easy to use as the electric kind, but getting the irrigation pipes to electricity would take longer."

As she put together what they said, Molly heard Adam get out of the truck. He circled around the cab. "Henry, do you have any heavy grease on hand? If so, and we apply it thick on the pipe and inside the sprinkler head threads, the new part will act the same as a threader. It'd take the same amount of effort and save you twenty bucks."

"I have a big can of grease for the tractor. Just the kind I think you mean," Henry said.

Rick grinned. "I never thought of that, Henry, but he could be right."

"Sorry, Rick. This is Adam Hollister, our new truck driver. Adam, Rick Canfield. He heads my irrigation crew. It's a full-time job," Molly added. "Listen, twenty dollars isn't much in the scheme of things. Would it be simpler to go buy a threader? It's warming up. We have fields needing water."

"Shouldn't take but a few minutes to try Adam's suggestion." Henry aimed his remark at Molly, who had yet to get out of the truck.

"Do it, then. Adam, you're technically off the clock. If you go along and give them a hand, list your additional hours and leave it on the office desk. Henry, I'll lock the barn. I plan to start hoeing weeds in the cabbage patch."

"Alone?" Henry glanced uneasily toward the south.

"I'll take Nitro."

"If you wait until morning, you can take Lana or Jesse along. Or both."

"In the morning I'm scheduled to show Adam the rest of the markets. Stop being such a worrywart, Henry. I'll be fine. You've forgotten how as a kid I ran wild to every corner of this ranch."

"Times have changed," he muttered. "Are you driving the long way around?"

She shook her head. "I thought I'd ride Cappy. He and Nitro can use the exercise. And if you're worried about stranger danger, I doubt any self-respecting thief will attack me for an old horse. All the same, I'll stake Nitro nearby."

"I know you're the boss now. And you think I'm fussy as a mother hen with chicks. But if I let anything happen to you, your daddy will come back and haunt me."

Molly crossed to Henry and gave him a hug. "I know you have my best interests at heart. Dad knew it, too. Things have changed here, I'm sorry to say. In fact, Adam staved off another incident today. I'll let him tell you about it while you three take care of the irrigation system. I'll have my cell phone, my police whistle, which you can hear for a mile, and my dog. Oh, and a hoe," she added, teasing her old friend. "I can wield a pretty mean hoe when push comes to shove. What more can I arm myself with?"

"Pepper spray." This came from Adam. "Some of the single women who frequented the bar carried three-ounce spray vials they told me you can buy off the internet."

"My girlfriend bought a mini stun gun in Mexico. She keeps it in her purse," Rick piped up.

Waving both hands as if to cancel out the last two suggestions, Molly said, "Now you're getting freaky. I'm a farmer, not Rambo. Get busy, you guys. Time is wasting." She signaled Nitro and entered the barn. Molly could hear the mumble of men's voices behind her. She hoped they were discussing re-threading sprinkler heads and not her.

She knew some not-so-good things had happened since she'd turned the ranch into gardens. Of course the area had grown and, in this stagnant economy, unemployment was high. People out of work got testy. She would take precautions, but not live in fear of what might be.

In the barn she saddled the Appaloosa

gelding her dad had bought when she was in high school. The horse was old now, his muzzle gray, but she hadn't been able to part with any of the horses when she'd sold off the cattle. She just needed more time to exercise all of them, or else pay an employee to help out.

The men were gone by the time she tied on the sling for her two hoes and got a running line for Nitro. With so few workers on the property in the afternoon she could probably let him run free beside Cappy. But the cabbage patch bordered a path where she'd seen signs of migrant travel. The path cut through her land, and might be why some folks in town felt she was complicit in border crossings.

The plot where she raised cabbage was the cultivated portion of her gardens nearest the river. She had adjacent land where she hoped to plant pecan trees or citrus. When she was a kid, markets carried local oranges and grapefruit. She'd learned winter freezes ruined a lot of the old crops. A few growers still experimented with varieties of hybrid oranges that had tougher skins than those grown in Florida and California. If cranberries proved to sell well, she could plant more of those in the boggy acres.

Riding through a valley that now lay fallow, Molly pictured lush rows of pecan and orange trees.

Her dad hadn't wanted her to plant anything this far from the house. Especially not cabbage, prominent in many Mexican dishes. He'd worried she'd lose half her crop to foragers. Now, as she sat atop Cappy surveying the rows, she saw holes, evidence her dad had been right.

She sighed, dismounted and led Cappy and Nitro to a grove of mesquite kept for their shade. It was plain from the discarded wrappers and water bottles that the grove was a stopping point for migrants. Molly loosened Cappy's saddle, tied the animals to branches then stopped to gather trash and stuff it into a garbage bag she'd brought for this purpose.

Whether the rows were rife with weeds or not, plainly she needed to get pickers out here tomorrow. The cabbage heads were a good size—those that hadn't been swiped.

Getting down to business, Molly clipped earbuds into her iPod and tucked it into a case strapped to her arm. She liked the mindless task of hoeing weeds. Time passed quickly when she worked to jazzy tunes. That was something she had missed, setting up farms in African villages. Only a few had sporadic satellite reception. Although by the time she left the corps, more places had service.

The sun beat down on her back. She took a break once, as the ball of heat moved into the west, and removed her long-sleeved shirt. She also got the animals and herself water. And she slathered sunscreen on areas exposed by her tank top.

The sounds of kids playing at the river meant school was out for the day. If she worked until dusk she might get through weeding one acre. If she assigned a crew of three or four out here, they'd finish the job in a single morning.

As weed after weed fell under her hoe she figured the labor costs against her time. It wouldn't hurt her. But the schools wanted her to add more classes. If she did, they'd need many more seedlings transferred out of the greenhouse. If she thought too far ahead, and tied those worries to her dwindling bank reserves, it gave her heartburn.

Brushing the worries away, she worked up and down rows for about an hour before pausing to rotate her shoulders and roll her head in a slow circle.

A long shadow fell across her from behind, giving Molly a heart-hammering start. She yanked out her earbuds and heard Nitro barking excitedly.

Gazing directly at the sun, even staring through sunglasses, it took her several panicked moments to identify Ranger, her father's black gelding.

For a split second Molly expected the broad-shouldered man in the saddle to be Mike McNair.

The knowledge it wasn't—couldn't be— made her squeeze back tears.

"Whoa there." Adam Hollister shortened the reins, bringing his mount to a full stop inches from her. "Henry sent me out to check on you. I figured you heard us. Nitro did," he said as he dismounted. "Are you okay?" he asked as he saw her edge aside her glasses and wipe her eyes with the back of one gloved hand.

"I—I…that's my dad's horse," she said before taking a deep breath.

"Sorry. It wasn't my idea to ride him. Like I said, Henry asked me to see how you were doing. He said the horse could use exercise."

"I can't deny that. Let's hike over and re-assure Nitro."

"Hey, did you clear all of these rows by yourself?" Adam swept a hand to indicate the weeds withering in the sun between cabbages. He took care to lead his mount between plant rows.

"It's not hard to make serious progress once you develop a rhythm." They reached the grove. Molly went down on one knee to calm her pet while Adam loosened the cinch on his saddle and tied his chuffing black mount to another mesquite. He took a bottle of water from his saddlebag and poured some into his cupped palm for Ranger.

"Henry should have had you bring a plastic bowl."

"He pointed me to the fridge in the barn

where you keep water. He probably thought I was smart enough to know I'd need a container."

Rising again, Molly smiled at Adam's self-deprecating comment. She liked a man able to admit shortcomings.

"As I rode up from the south, I noticed some plants had the heads lopped off. Is that how you harvest cabbage, in fits and spurts?"

"That's how people stealing from me pick cabbage. I'll send pickers down here in the morning. Say, did you guys attach the sprinkler heads okay?"

"We did. Whoever took the old heads only bent one pipe to where we had to cut it back and re-groove it. That took us the longest." Adam knelt and picked up a broken branch. He dug down four or five inches in several spots between two rows.

"What are you doing?" Molly frowned at him.

Dropping the stick, he stood and dusted off his hands. "Uh, this is really black soil. I wondered if it was naturally wet, like if it's fed from an underground spring or something."

"My dad said this area often used to flood, leaving behind rich, black silt. It's rare now for floodwaters to stretch this far. Dad had this land sown in sweet grass he cut to feed cattle. Listen, I need to get back to work. You can go back and tell Henry I'm fine, and he should go on home."

"I see you have an extra hoe. Why don't I give you a hand?"

"I pay you trucker's wages, but only for four hours a day. Since you helped with the irrigation piping, I already owe you more today." She shaded her eyes to look at him.

Adam opened his mouth, presumably to respond. But a commotion in the direction of the river, accompanied by high-pitched cries for help, killed whatever he'd been about to say.

Molly dropped her hoe and took off running over the weeds she'd cut.

A moment behind her, Adam soon caught up. "Are they playing or is someone really in trouble?" His voice jerked between pants.

She shook her head. When they reached

the end of the rows, they could see a small group of young boys huddled at the water's edge, some running downriver screaming for help. Molly doubled her pace.

Still, Adam was first to reach the boys in wet cut-offs. They were shivering in spite of the afternoon heat. "What happened?" he called.

One kid pointed toward those loping along the riverbank. "We were diving for a tennis ball, and Bobby Parks must've hit his head on a log or somethin'. He came up, his face bloody. And the river took him. Look." The boy pointed.

"Where do you kids live?" she asked as she tried to catch her breath. The boys jerked a thumb away from her property to an area where she knew there were a cluster of cottages that once housed cowboys working various cattle ranches. "One of you go get Bobby's mom or dad," she ordered, realizing Adam had taken off again.

He stripped off his shirt, then his boots and socks, as he stumbled downriver over flat rocks to where she now saw bobbing along what she hoped was the injured boy in the river. Then the boy sank from sight and she didn't see him pop up again.

With her heart in her throat, she ran after Adam, scooping up his fallen clothing as she went. He made a running dive into the muddy water. And she didn't breathe until he surfaced with the boy. The water was swifter in the center of the river. Adam didn't have an easy task getting himself and a gangly youth back to shore.

But he managed.

Running to where he staggered out of the water, it crossed Molly's mind that had she been alone, she may not have been able to rescue the now limp boy.

The kid, drained of color, had a bump in the center of his forehead, with a cut beginning to trickle blood.

Molly fell to her knees still clutching Adam's belongings. He laid the kid down and started CPR. A ring of wide-eyed boys in various shades from sunburned red to nut brown stood in silence, expressions anxious.

The boy on the ground jerked a few times, coughed and spit up a stream of water. He blinked and tried to sit up. Only then did Adam ease back on his heels. His eyes met Molly's and they both heaved big sighs.

One boy from the first group raced toward them from farther downriver. At his heels ran a woman carrying a toddler.

"That dude saved Bobby Jim," one of the kids announced. The woman fell to her knees, gathered up Bobby and sobbed out her thanks.

Molly stared with frank admiration at her new employee, who seemed embarrassed by the attention and the praise.

CHAPTER FIVE

ADAM ROSE FROM his crouch and skirted the reunion. He bent next to Molly, who still clutched his discarded clothing, and separated his T-shirt from his shoes. Shaking out the shirt, he rubbed it over his dripping hair then tugged it over his head.

Still on her knees, Molly's eyes tracked two drops of water running down his suntanned chest before he slowly unrolled the shirt hem down his still-damp torso. Her hands tightened around his socks and boots in a move so unconscious Adam had to pry them away from her.

"Oh, sorry," she said belatedly, loosening her grip. She marveled at how easily he put on the socks and boots without having to sit.

"Everything's okay here," he said, shaking his wet hair. "We should get back to the horses and Nitro, and let Mrs. Parks get

Bobby to a doctor." He extended a hand to help Molly up.

"Right." She grasped the tips of his fingers, still cool from his dip in the river, and surged to her feet. She managed to smile at a scrawny boy who ran up.

"You guys saved Bobby," the boy blurted, his dark eyes filling his thin face. "If you own the cabbage patch, me and some others stole some. I'm sorry. I promise I won't do it anymore."

Bobby's mother straightened, too. "Are you Ms. McNair?" The woman hoisted the toddler higher on her hip. "My husband used to work for your dad. Eldon stayed on after Mike took sick and some of the wranglers left to find other jobs. He probably stayed too long. With ranch jobs scarce, it was only last month that he hired on at Junior Henderson's ranch.

"We—uh, he hated to see you let the cattle go. But my kids are part of the school's Friday backpack food program. Their teachers said we have you to thank for the fresh produce. And now you saved Bobby's life." Her lips trembled as did the hand she kept running through her son's curly wet hair. "How can I thank you?"

"I didn't save him, Mrs. Parks. Adam did. I hate to think what might have happened if he hadn't ridden out to see how I was coming along hoeing weeds today. I'm not sure I could've managed to get Bobby to shore if I'd been alone."

Bobby's mother made a sweeping glance of the kids now crowding around her son. "Yes, well, I thought the boys were pitching quarters at Paul Valenzuela's house."

All of the boys had the grace to look guilty. Bobby, still hoarse from his ordeal, said, "I don't want to see a doctor, Mama. It was hot. We were bored. Paul's big brother said he'd come with us, but his girlfriend came over and they went off to do homework."

Adam didn't involve himself in the conversation. In fact, Molly realized he had left and was walking back to the field. She thought he might have stayed and impressed on the boys the dangers of swimming unsupervised. But maybe he felt they'd learned their lesson.

"I'm glad it ended well, Mrs. Parks," Molly murmured. "But you should have Bobby checked out." Pausing to settle her gaze on the kid who admitted to taking her cabbages, she added, "Stealing from some-one is never acceptable. Next time you or your friends want cabbage, or other vege-tables for your moms, find me or one of my crew. We'll pick some for you."

"You're too kind, Ms. McNair." Bobby's mother lowered her eyes and her voice. "Sometimes the paycheck doesn't stretch to serving three meals a day. We'll do bet-ter now that Eldon is working again. Some folks aren't so lucky." She didn't single out any particular boy, but because her gaze lin-gered on a couple of kids, one being the boy who'd admitted to stealing cabbage, Molly identified some who might need more as-sistance.

She vowed to check with the school. Since she knew where these kids lived, it shouldn't be hard to deduce who needed extra food. But she would have to tread lightly. Her dad often said families here who'd fallen on hard times were proud folks. He said most would work three jobs rather than accept charity. "I, uh, need to go back to hoeing weeds," she said.

"The boys should go home and get hoes and help you," Mrs. Parks said.

"Oh, that isn't necessary. They're all shaken up."

Mrs. Parks' eyes grew glassy with tears again. "I'll take Bobby to the clinic." She motioned for the whole pack of boys to head home.

Molly turned in the opposite direction. Before she made it back to where she'd dropped her hoe she saw Adam pick it up.

"Adam, what are you doing? You must be uncomfortable working in those soaking wet jeans."

"They'll dry," he said without turning.

"How can you work? I'm still shaky from witnessing that boy's accident."

Gripping the hoe, Adam turned. "You think I'm fine? I thought the kid had drowned. The river was so murky I was lucky to locate him."

Molly couldn't see Adam's eyes because

of his sunglasses, but his knuckles and a circle around his lips looked white.

"I know. I saw him bob up once, then he sank out of sight." She shivered. "You know something... I'm ready to call it a day. Weeding doesn't seem important."

"You came here to clear weeds. There's nothing we can do to rewind the tape of that accident. He's lucky. Hopefully those kids will be more careful."

"I agree, but the day is winding down. I have chores I can do away from sight and sound of the river, which at the moment is a stark reminder." Molly took her hoe out of his hands and walked over to her horse where she slid the tool into the sling hanging from the saddle.

"You're the boss." Adam went to his horse. Nitro got up, shook, yawned a massive yawn and trotted up to Adam. "Do you let him loose to run home?" he asked as he finished tightening the cinch on his saddle.

"No. I probably could, as the workers have all left for the day. But I worry all the same. If he bit someone passing through my property I'd feel terrible." She unclipped the dog's lead line from the tree then checked that the lobster-claw hook remained solidly attached to Nitro's collar.

Adam swung into his saddle. The leather around the cantle turned dark from his wet jeans.

"I still have some of my dad's clothes at the house. You're welcome to try a pair of his jeans. I think they'd fit you."

Ranger had jogged out ahead of Molly's mount. Adam reined him in and let her catch up. "I might take you up on that offer. I have a twenty-minute ride home on my bike after I take care of the horse."

"Is the job worth traveling forty minutes a day?"

Adam darted a glance her way. "Seems we've had this conversation before. To be honest, I've never worked for anyone who offered me so many reasons why I should quit. Have I done something to offend you?"

"No. I can't figure you out."

"What's to figure? You advertised for a truck driver at a time the job with my friend ended. I live rent-free in a travel trailer parked on his property. I can afford to work less and fish more." He shot her a grin.

"Sounds like the life for someone who's semiretired, not an able-bodied fortysome-thing guy."

"So it bothers you that I'm not more ambitious?"

She gave a nervous little cough. "That's none of my business," she said and kicked Cappy into a slow canter that startled Nitro who had been sniffing in an empty rabbit hole. He loped to catch up. By the time they reached the ranch, his tongue was hanging out.

ADAM COULD HAVE passed Molly given he had the younger, longer-legged horse. But he held Ranger back and mulled over whether she instinctively didn't trust him because he had taken the job under false pretenses. Maybe because she was nothing like what he expected, unconsciously his guilt was getting to him.

Really, though, he hadn't come to hurt her. If he found her farm sat on a boatload of oil, the outfit Dave worked for would dicker with her over leasing rights. He just knew from experience that big oil guys often wanted something for nothing. He could hang around and look out for Molly's interests. That thought made him feel better as he followed her to the barn where she dismounted and unhooked Nitro.

"That made for a nice run," he said, climbing from his saddle. She'd already opened the doors to the barn where the animals were housed and was hanging the hoe on wall pegs where Adam saw an array of farm tools.

"I'll take care of grooming and putting up the horses if you'd like to run up to the house and change into dry jeans." She fished a key out of her pocket. "My dad's room is at the back of the house. There are two open boxes on the bed. One is filled with jeans, the other with shirts. Just go to the end of the hall you'll face when you walk in. Oh, and if you wouldn't mind taking Nitro, he has food and water in the kitchen."

Adam hesitantly took the key she held out. "You're sure you're okay sending someone who's practically a stranger into your home?"

"I guess the gallop jarred some sense into me. You saved my expensive truck and maybe my life today by your quick thinking. You saved Bobby at the river when you had no idea how bad the current might be. Instead of giving you the third degree about why you took my part-time job, I should be thanking you."

She glanced away from him and shrugged.

"My dad never owned anything worth stealing except for his cattle. And a person who joins the Peace Corps…well, it's practically like taking a vow of poverty. Don't expect to see anything of worth in the house."

Waving him off, she collected the reins to both horses.

"Okay. Do you want me to bring Nitro back here after I change?"

"Sure. I like to have him nearby when I work around the place alone."

Adam set off then turned back. "By the way, thanks for the loan of your dad's clothes. I'll see they get washed and returned."

"No need. I'm taking the boxes to a charity. I haven't made time to do it yet. Frankly it speaks to a finality I haven't yet been able to embrace."

Adam nodded because a lump had risen in his throat. He'd had to deal with the same thing. In truth he hadn't managed it well. He'd called a company that handled estate sales. A friend had recommended them. The three women had cataloged and marked everything in the house except for his clothing.

He'd donated what money the sale earned above and beyond the estate people's fee, to the children's hospital.

Funds from selling the house went to an opera company Jennifer had loved. Dave had said he'd only donated to them because he couldn't sit still through an opera and felt guilty over staying abroad to keep from buying a season ticket for himself.

Maybe so.

Heaven knew he'd had reasons enough to whip himself with guilt.

He hurried up to the house, the dog beside him.

Inside it was cool and dark. As his eyes

adjusted, he heard Nitro bound into what had to be the kitchen, because of the sound of lapping water followed by crunching kibble. He took a moment to study the living room. It fit his general notion of a ranch house. The large room held oversize dark leather furniture. The high ceiling had exposed beams and a center wagon-wheel chandelier with six lantern lights.

A massive stone fireplace with a weathered wood mantel drew him closer. Adam wasn't surprised to see an array of family photos. One was of a wedding couple—probably Molly's parents. A smaller frame was of a smiling woman holding an infant—obviously the baby was Molly since the trail of frames from there on were of her as a toddler, then gap-toothed and grinning atop a pony, then on a younger version of the horse she'd ridden today with a backdrop of cattle. There was also a photo taken on the porch of her with an older man. They were both dressed in Western wear, and the resemblance told Adam how much Molly favored her dad. The last two wooden frames held photos of her in graduation gowns. Given the difference in age and color of the gowns, Adam judged one to be from high school and the other from college.

He carefully set the frame down and turned away. Striding down the hall, he wished he hadn't stopped to see the McNair legacy so neatly laid out.

It opened a pit in his stomach.

If he'd skipped that one last job he hadn't needed, to make a simple trip with his family, his daughter's growth would be recorded in photos across his own fireplace mantel.

He found the room, bare except for a stripped bed and dresser. The open boxes of clothing were on the bed as Molly had said they'd be. He unfolded the top pair of well-worn jeans, shook them out and held them up to him. They looked as if they'd fit. Molly had a good eye.

Regardless of the fact he was alone in the house except for Nitro, Adam felt uneasy shucking his jeans and underwear with the door wide open. The bedroom had an en suite bath. He stepped inside, shut the door and pulled off his boots and socks for the second time that afternoon. Peeling out of wet jeans and shorts was harder. He looked around for a towel, but the bathroom had also been stripped.

He rolled his shorts into a bundle with his wet jeans that smelled like the river, and yanked on the borrowed pants. They did fit, and he appreciated the much-laundered fabric against his chafed skin. He took another moment to thread his belt through the loops and wasted no time restoring his socks and boots.

He gathered his wet things, left the bathroom and met Nitro in the hall. "Hey, buddy, did you eat your fill? If so, we'd better get going or your mistress will be wondering if I am ransacking her house. I know she said there's nothing here worth stealing. That's an understatement. The Western art hanging along the hall wall is nothing to sneeze at."

Nitro woofed and sniffed the hem of one leg of the borrowed jeans Adam had let hang loose over the tops of his boots. "I guess you recognize the smell, huh? I hope you don't take a chunk out of my hide when I try to leave the house wearing something that doesn't belong to me."

The dog stuck close to Adam's side as they made their way to the barn.

Adam crossed to his Harley and stuffed the wet clothing in one of the saddlebags. Turning back, he entered the barn.

Molly had finished brushing Cappy. He'd been returned to his stall, where he raised his head from the oat trough to whicker when Nitro and Adam breezed in.

"Here's your house key," Adam said, holding it out to Molly. With his other hand he took the brush out of hers. "I got back in time to groom Ranger. Off the clock," he added.

She shook her head and laughed. "That's not what I was going to say."

"Maybe not, but you were about to refuse my help. I know horses. I grew up in Fort Worth around horses. As a kid when I rode, the drill was, you ride, you groom the horse and see he has a clean stall."

"Generally that's true here, too. But in this case I don't mind. And if you leave now chances are you'll avoid rush-hour traffic."

"I've yet to see what I'd consider rush-hour traffic." Adam stroked Ranger's arched neck and then ran the brush over his withers and beyond to his tail. Long strokes the gelding seemed to enjoy.

Molly turned over a bucket and sat on it. Nitro scampered up and nudged her with his head until she scratched his ears. "Do you still get to ride horses? You're efficient at grooming."

Adam glanced around at her. "My friend who owns the bar has four horses. I probably ride them as much as his family does. When I go fishing."

"Ah, you really fish. Okay, I'll let you finish up with Ranger. You know which stall is his. I put his ration of oats in the trough. Nitro and I have some transplanting to do from one of the greenhouses. Would you make sure this barn door is locked when you leave?"

"If you'll hang on until I'm done, I'd like to see your greenhouse."

"Greenhouses. I started with one, but I have two now."

"Well, I've never been inside one. But maybe you don't have time to let me tag along."

"If you truly are interested I'll be glad

to show you around. Greenhouse work is muggy and boring, but having them makes controlling the growing seasons easier. I have a crew that helps when the seeds arrive, but I'm generally responsible for all crop rotation."

"There, this guy is all spiffed up. Where shall I put the brush?" he asked, looking around.

"It goes on that empty peg next to the row of bridles." Molly opened a stall door and the big black gelding went in on his own.

"My friend could take some lessons. His barn is a mess."

Molly laughed. "Credit for all of the organization here goes to my dad and Henry. Type A's. You probably didn't go into the kitchen, but it's the same. When I was growing up we couldn't keep a cook because Dad roared if the salsa so much as got shifted around in the fridge."

"Wow. I thought by nature men were slobs." Adam gave a small, one-sided smile and fell into step with Molly as she left the barn.

"Not the McNair men. Henry says my grandpa wanted to walk into the barn and tell at a glance if anything was missing. He died shortly after I was born, so I never knew him. From the stories, he was a character."

"So he started the ranch and your father inherited from him?" Nitro walked between them.

"Yes. My grandfather's parents owned a meat-packing company outside Corpus Christi. Are you familiar with that area?"

"I know where it is."

"My grandfather was a twin. Neither of them wanted to work in the packing plant, so they scouted out cheap land—that's what this was back in the day. They bought this acreage then worked as cowhands and built a herd little by little."

Adam nodded as they walked. "So how did it just end up in your dad's possession?"

"My great-grandfather was killed in a loading accident. My great-grandmother needed one of the boys to return home to run the business."

"Ah, I see. So your grandfather wanted to stay and ranch."

"They both wanted to stay." She shook

her head. "They had a friend shuffle a deck of cards then the brothers each cut a section. Low card holder had to run the packing plant, the other got the ranch."

Molly unlocked the greenhouse and rows of lights came on automatically. Nitro flopped down beside the door.

"That's a remarkable story," Adam said, stopping to look at the long rows of tables filled with flats of small pots. "Guys I know would want to draw again for best out of three. Who'd so willingly consign himself to a lifetime of work he hated based strictly on chance?"

"They were brothers—they must've loved each other." Molly shrugged. "Back then a man's word meant something. And my dad was always quick to point out that his uncle made a fortune at the meat plant. He retired early to travel the world, while Grandpa struggled to get a herd through drought, declining meat prices and rising land taxes."

"Was he happy?"

Molly glanced up from pulling on a pair of leather gloves. "I don't know. Do men discuss happiness?" She held up a hand. "I'm not being sexist. I don't think I ever heard my dad or his friends or my friends mention emotions. At least from my limited contact with the guys who live around here and raise cattle. Most spoke of having a successful year or success in their work. Okay, so this is what a greenhouse looks like."

Adam delivered her a long look. "Interesting. Are you happy doing what you do?" He hooked his thumbs in his back pockets and slowly took in what she'd started doing— moving small square cardboard boxes, each holding a plant of some kind, into an empty wooden flat she took from a stack under the table.

"I love seeing a plant sprout from a tiny seed and grow to where it produces a vegetable or fruit. For instance, these will one day blossom and form a squash." Molly held up two containers. "This one will give me yellow squash and this one zucchini. If all goes well once I plant them outside, you'll be hauling them to market sometime in August."

Adam noticed she hadn't said she was happy.

Happiness certainly wasn't anything he'd felt in a while. But as he looked back on his life he did think at the height of his business success, knowing he'd provided well for his family had made him happy.

And then the success had gotten too important.

"Are you planning to plant all of these little guys today?" He watched as she filled a flat and set it on an oversize flatbed wagon. "It seems like double work."

"I told you, crop—"

"Controlling crop rotation, right. I guess I've always subscribed to the philosophy of not handling a single item more than once." He picked up a wooden flat and began to fill it as she was doing.

"I'll plant what I can. Thanks for wanting to help, but you don't have gloves."

"I've been dirtier. And I wash," he said, shooting her a smile. "Unless you're the type of person who doesn't want others messing in."

"No. No. I have workers who help. I'm still feeling my way with financing the farm. Transplanting is easy enough once I get in a rhythm. So far I've done it mostly by myself. If I decide to plant citrus and nut trees, I'll pay to have that done."

Adam bent to set his filled flat beside hers on the wagon. "Take advantage of the free labor this evening. I'll tag along. Supposing I can learn the next step, I'll help getting squash—is it?—in the ground."

"Okay, but it'll use muscles you might not have used in a while. I'll still expect you to show up on time in the morning to drive the truck to the next day-markets."

"How hard can it be?" he muttered, starting on another flat as Molly rolled over another wagon.

They worked well together and the wagons were soon filled. "I'll pull these to wherever you're going to plant. Then I'll go get a pair of gloves from my bike."

"I hope they're ones you don't mind ruining. They may not survive a siege of planting."

"That's okay. I have others."

He also had vials in his saddlebags for taking soil samples. This might be his opportunity and, frankly, he wanted to get it over with.

They pulled the wagons out of the greenhouse and up the road. "This is far enough," Molly said. "The squash goes in the children's garden."

"Great. It's handy to where I parked the Harley. Give me a minute to go get my gloves."

At his bike he pulled out his gloves and suffered momentary doubt when he tucked a needle-thin extendable probe and two glass vials into the pocket of his borrowed jeans.

He hated going behind Molly's back. She wasn't the ogre Dave Benson had made her out to be. She was a hard worker and generous to a fault. That impressed him. And something about sneaking around left a bad taste in his mouth.

Not only that—it was probably pointless to check her land for possible oil when it was unlikely she'd ever partner with Branchville Oil.

And yet earlier, in passing, she'd made an oblique reference to finances. An oil well or two could alleviate her money woes if funding her farm was an issue.

Grappling a moment, but having more or less rationalized his part in an outcome that in the end would totally be between Molly and Branchville, he returned to help transplant squash.

He didn't think he'd been gone long, but Molly already had half her plants in a neat row in the ground.

"What happened to the cardboard cartons?" Adam asked, peering down at her empty trays.

"They're a great invention. The cup is biodegradable and has a fertilizer pressed into the paper. As we water, the containers disintegrate and feed the plants until they've rooted. All you need to do is dig holes deep enough to bury the pots. Place them about ten inches apart."

He nodded. "Shall I start a new row?" Maybe he wouldn't get to take a sample, after all.

"Why don't you go to the end of the one I'm working on and plant toward me? That

way if we work until dark we won't leave
two partial rows."

Hallelujah!

He rolled his wagon to where she'd
marked the end of the row with a stake. She
was making it way too easy for him to sample the soil.

Removing the first bit of earth as he'd
watched her do, he found it dark and damp—
one positive sign. His device worked on a
plunger that sent a high-tech tweezer probe
two feet into the ground. It retracted and
he quickly transferred bits of soil into his
two vials and buttoned them into his shirt
pocket. At first glance he thought maybe
the chemist Branchville had hired to give
an opinion on this land's oil viability might
be right.

Nitro trotted over and laid at his feet.
Adam took off one glove and scratched the
dog between his ears. Then he settled down
to work. He had thought planting would be a
snap, but Molly appeared at his side to give
him some tips for speeding up and keeping
a straight line. Then she planted what re-

mained of his wagon load in half the time it took him.

After bringing out three more wagons each, Adam thought back to his earlier muttered comment about how hard could transplanting be and was forced to admit he might suffer mightily from aching muscles come morning.

He was relieved when Molly eventually said, "Are you ready to call it a day? We could plant two more wagon loads before dark, but it'd be iffy. You did well for a novice farmer," she said, grinning when Adam joined her and stood rotating his shoulders in a lame attempt to ease his sore back.

"I think you're part robot," he said, peeling off his dirt-caked gloves. "Do you plant like this every day?"

"Vegetable gardening runs in cycles. I don't put in twelve hours every day, but with gardens this size, I keep busy." She whistled for Nitro, who bounded to her side. "Hey, I had a thought. Are you hungry? The least I can do to repay you for all of your assistance is drag a couple of steaks out of the freezer and toss them on the barbecue. It won't take long to fix a salad. And I have a specialty bread I can grill. A friend made it fresh yesterday. She sells the tastiest bread you'll ever eat at some of the same markets I go to. You may meet her tomorrow."

The offer of food sounded tempting. However, Adam didn't want to chance having her see the outline of the vials in his shirt pocket and ask an offhanded question he couldn't answer.

"I may have a hard time getting out of bed. I think I'll go home and take a long shower."

"Sure. It was just a thought." She bent and snatched up the tongues of both wagons. "You can take off now. I'll stow this gear and close the greenhouse. Nitro," she said in a commanding voice, "hop on the wagon."

Adam was surprised by how easily the big dog complied. Watching the pair melt into the gathering twilight, he felt guiltier still for turning her down. It may have seemed that she extended the invitation lightly, but for some reason he didn't think she made a habit of asking her employees to eat with her.

Before he could change his mind, he

strode to his bike, stowed his gloves, slung a leg over the seat and kicked the engine to life.

It was full dark by the time he rolled up to his even blacker trailer behind the bar where a few vehicles were still parked out front. He climbed off the seat, stifling a groan brought on by his already aching muscles. He had his key in his hand before he turned off the headlamp.

The light no more than winked out when he was slammed from front and back. Shocked by the jolt, he realized he'd been jumped by two burly men. Not one to go down easily, he butted his head into the front assailant while jabbing his elbow hard backward.

He heard a grunt only seconds before his feet were kicked out from under him. A boot that felt the size of Paul Bunyan's ground against his chest, pinning him like a bug in a display case. He heard the glass vials in his pocket crack and felt shards of glass pierce his skin. "If this is a robbery," he managed to growl, "I've only got ten bucks on me.

And there's no money inside. Take the keys to the Harley. It's vintage."

"Shut up," one man snarled. "We ought to rough you up for knocking us off the road. We're only trying to scare the woman into selling our boss her land. And it looks like you're helping her farm instead."

"Boss?" Adam's mind scrambled. "You mean Dave?"

The boot that had stomped on Adam's chest lifted but smacked his right cheekbone so hard it spun his head to the side.

"Don't know any Dave. You're supposed to be sniffing out oil. The boss needs an answer ASAP. If you don't have a report in two weeks, we'll meet again, hotshot. Next time we might break a few bones."

Adam lay still, trying his best to catch a glimpse of the pair. Both wore black and blended with the night. He heard them stalk away. Touching the spot on his face that felt numb, he slowly sat up.

Car doors slammed in the vicinity of the bar. He staggered to his feet, wanting to see what type of vehicle they drove. But he felt woozy. And they'd peeled out by the time he steadied himself with a hand on his bike, which oddly had remained upright.

So, he assumed, they must work for Branchville. Navigating the few steps to his door, he again felt the sting of broken glass prick his chest.

The two claimed they didn't know Dave. But he sure did. And he'd make it clear to his former partner that these jokers had ruined the samples that could have given them the answers they'd wanted.

Did Dave know the kind of men he was dealing with?

Adam was through.

Dave could pass that on or not.

Now, though, Adam was worried for Molly.

CHAPTER SIX

MOLLY WONDERED WHATEVER had possessed her to invite Adam Hollister to dinner. What did she know about the man, really? Only what was on his application. If for no other reason than that, she should keep him at a distance until she knew him better. Even if he did intrigue her as few men had.

Although, as fast as he turned down her casual dinner invitation, either he was afraid she'd planned to put moves on him or he'd found her a few eggs short of an omelet.

It was hard to admit, but rattling around in the big family home too often left her lonely. She never felt it more acutely than during an evening meal.

That was one reason she worked such long hours.

Tonight, after tidying the greenhouse, she made her way to the house to fix another solitary supper. She skipped thawing a steak. Instead she prepared a salad and a toasted slice of Tess's dark rye bread.

For noise, she flipped on the kitchen TV to a news station. But it was all so depressing, she snapped the set off again.

Adam was hard to read, which could be the very thing that piqued her interest. It didn't hurt that he was easy on the eyes. She stopped eating. Good looks were nice, but she'd never been one to put too much stock in them. For a man to appeal to her he needed to be kind. And honest. And have a sense of humor.

He'd also need to recognize the value of her gardens. Was that being too picky?

How silly was she—daydreaming about attributes for a significant someone in her life? She didn't frequent places where single men hung out. So why waste her time on the subject because Adam Hollister had turned down her offer of a simple meal?

Truthfully it was because his refusal left her facing another evening alone in a long line of them. To be really honest, she'd never liked being alone. It went back to her childhood. She had longed to be part of a big family and used to confide in her horse that one day she'd get married and have a lot of kids. At thirty-two that chance was growing dimmer. She just needed to appreciate her farm family—the loyal men and women who worked for her, cared about her.

She finished her salad and got up to rinse the plate. One of her dad's favorite sayings popped into her head: no use crying over spilled milk.

She settled the house for the night and went off to bed. Instead of reading the love story she'd started a few days ago, she chose a gardening magazine. She was soon lost in a series of articles on the number of organic farmers quitting the business because of a tightening of FDA rules. That didn't cheer her up.

Molly closed the magazine and shut off her light. Tonight it seemed she was doomed to not go to sleep with happy thoughts. Then she heard the reassuring clink of Nitro's dog tags as he settled on his bed.

She really wasn't alone. The next best

thing to having a man in her life was having man's best friend.

That let her snuggle in with a smile.

MUTED STREAKS OF sunlight peeking between the blinds woke Molly prior to her alarm going off. She stretched and the magazine she'd been reading when she went to bed fell to the floor. The noise startled Nitro. He leaped up and landed on the errant magazine, barking his head off.

"Good dog. You captured the offender." She laughed and bent to give him a head rub. "Since we're both awake, let's get breakfast." Straightening, Molly shut off her alarm.

By the time she finished her morning routine, she looked out the kitchen window and saw her pickers arriving. She snapped a leash on Nitro and hurried out to greet them and start the day, staking Nitro out in his favorite spot in the shade.

Molly was surprised to learn they'd all heard about yesterday's rescue of Bobby Parks. Luisa Estrada, usually so quiet and reticent, spontaneously hugged Molly. "It could have been any of our sons. We tell them, don't go to the river without an adult, but they sneak off anyway."

Gena Munoz rallied. "Seeing Bobby almost drown shook my Carlos. Maybe he won't be so quick to follow his friends to the river."

Carlotta Valenzuela nodded. "My son, Paul, didn't tell me. My husband heard it from Bobby's dad after they saw the doctor. Paul finally admitted if you hadn't been there to save Bobby, Molly, he'd have drowned. According to him it all happened so fast, the boys didn't know what to do."

"Wait, I didn't save Bobby. My new driver, Adam, dived into the river and brought him out and did CPR. I was as slow off the mark as the kids were."

The women began talking to one another in Spanish. "Sorry," Gena said, reverting to English. "I recall Carlos mentioned that a man pulled Bobby from the river. He also said you sent him after Bobby's mom. When I called her to check on Bobby, it was you she praised."

"I guess because Adam isn't well known.

And he didn't stick around to collect his thanks."

"The man's a hero."

"He'll be here soon to load the truck. The markets open in a few hours." Molly produced the keys to her SUV and called over Gena, one of her most trusted employees. "Will you take three other women to the cabbage patch to cut heads from the two rows I weeded yesterday? Fill yellow crates. I think they'll all fit in the back. Luisa and Carlotta are most familiar with banding and packing romaine, so leave them here."

Some workers left, others returned to their rows to pull carrots and pick tomatoes and cucumbers. The crates began to fill up.

Molly hopped across rows to check the squash plants she and Adam had transplanted. With the sun heating up earlier in the day, the leaves were starting to wilt. She went to the barn to call Rick and have him add the new bed to the morning irrigation circuit.

She came out as Adam rolled in on his noisy bike. She detoured to where he was parking, thinking she ought to forewarn him that he might be bombarded with praise from the women for yesterday's deed.

"Hi," she called, walking up behind him. "The local grapevine was busy last night. Expect to get a lot of hugs from the pickers for saving Bobby Parks from drowning."

Adam spun around to face her and it was a full moment before Molly reacted in shock to his injured eye. "Adam! How did you get that shiner?"

He gingerly touched a finger to the puffy, black-and-blue flesh. "I can think of two stock answers. One, I ran into a door in the dark. Or, two, you should see the other guy."

Molly didn't laugh, so Adam shifted uncomfortably. "It pains me more to admit I didn't fare so well against the two bruisers who jumped me from behind when I got home last night. Probably the hazard of renting a trailer behind a bar," he muttered, all the while feeling guilty for avoiding the truth.

"Were you robbed?"

"No. I told them up front I only had ten bucks on me and nothing worth stealing in the trailer. I must not have looked too prosperous. They got in a few licks and ran off."

Moving nearer, Molly studied his injury with a frown. "The purple bruise under your eye is shaped like a boot heel. Were they cowboys? Did you call the police?"

"It was too dark to see them. They didn't steal anything. I didn't call the cops. I went inside and went to bed with a bag of frozen peas taped over my eye. I'm fine to work." Turning his back on her, he pulled a new pair of gloves out of his saddlebag.

She had more questions, but Henry drove in. He was soon commiserating with Adam. Then the men excused themselves to look at a tractor repair Henry wanted Adam's advice on.

"I'll be back to load the truck in a few minutes," he told Molly. Unsaid but implied by the low grate of his voice was that she shouldn't start loading crates on her own.

She tossed her head. He acted pretty high-handed for an employee. A new one, at that. She didn't know how she felt about Henry suddenly getting all BFF with him.

Who'd made Adam the go-to person for equipment repairs?

Shaking it off, she headed back to the garden to start stacking crates that would go to market. Uppermost in her thoughts—she was afraid the uneasy knot in the pit of her stomach stemmed from worrying whether or not she was the cause of Adam's attack. Were the men who jumped him the same ones who'd beaten Ramon?

Deputy Powell had intimated there were men who didn't like that she'd gotten rid of her dad's cattle. That made no sense to her. Her dad shipped cattle to markets, and the beef ended up on consumer's dinner tables. Was that so different from her operation?

She wasn't so naïve that she didn't understand the feud in some minds stretching back to the territorial war. Just because she was color blind when it came to hunger didn't mean everyone was. Henry and Alma hadn't been treated well when they'd first settled in Laredo. Still, it was hard for Molly to fathom why any sane adult would resent feeding hungry people, especially children.

Much subdued from her earlier joy at facing a new morning, she began to haul full crates of vegetables to the spot where Adam would park the truck. Which he soon did.

As she'd predicted, the pickers rushed over to thank him for saving Bobby. She smiled, watching his attempts to shuck off the praise. Even more interesting was observing how red he turned when Gena and others clucked over his black eye and offered home remedies to help reduce the swelling, such as lying down with a warm teabag over his injury. They appeared to think he'd been hurt during the rescue.

He managed to thank them for their good wishes and suggestions, but dived right into loading the truck.

Molly said nothing as they worked.

"I'm not used to so much mothering," he said to her in a loud whisper.

"I think I should let you go," she blurted, frowning up at him.

"Let me go?" Adam straightened to stare down at her from his good eye.

Had someone tipped her off that he was here to scout her land for oil?

He vaulted off the truck to stand at her

level. He still looked down on her from his superior height, however. "You mean…fire me?"

"What if I'm the reason you were attacked last night?"

He tensed. "How so?" he asked.

She crossed her arms and rubbed both elbows with her worn gloves. "You're my third driver who's been jumped by bullies. Men I'm beginning to think may object to the fact I don't discriminate when it comes to who I feed. In other words, I don't ask to see papers on the parents of the children in the backpack program.

"Something Officer Powell said when Ramon was harassed makes me think there may be an organized group who resent any part I play in feeding schoolkids whose parents could be undocumented. A group who'd like my farm to fail. Maybe they're squeamish about attacking me overtly. At least, nothing happened to me the days between when Ramon quit and I hired you. I delivered produce to markets in my SUV. I could drive the truck," she said, eyeing the big Ford with some misgiving.

RELIEVED, ADAM QUICKLY set the next four crates onto the truck and vaulted up to stack them in order. There could well be people who objected to her giving food away. He'd heard some such grumblers at the bar. But he'd paid scant attention to their griping. Really, they were penny ante compared to the more powerful outfit that wanted her land for oil to add to their already hefty profits. Those were the people he suspected. And he didn't like it.

He also didn't like that he'd tried to phone Dave Benson, only to learn the number he'd given Adam was not in service. Last night's debacle had the opposite effect from what he was sure the Branchville executives wanted. They wanted his cooperation and they wanted it yesterday. Because if Dave's information was correct, the time to qualify for the government contract for matching funds was passing.

Negotiating was one thing, bullying quite another.

Adam fully intended to run Dave to ground and make the guy answer to his suspicions. He needed to know if Molly faced a few disgruntled locals who might see her farm as responsible for their unemployment or if the top brass at the oil company was behind the intimidation tactics.

He'd always run his company on the up-and-up. Farmers and oilmen could coexist without strong-arm tactics. He'd have no part in that.

"Hand me more crates," he said to Molly. "You could be jumping to conclusions. The guys I had my run-in with left when I said I had nothing of value."

Molly automatically retrieved another set of full crates. "So you don't think it was related to the earlier incident out on the on ramp? Or that they might be the same men who roughed up Ramon?"

Adam wished she'd quit digging—quit brooding. He didn't like lying to her. "Are we falling behind the pickers?" he finally ventured, hoping to divert her attention.

"Yikes. Yes." She rushed to catch up. Returning to the truck with two crates, she sat them at Adam's feet.

He plucked a purple vegetable out of the top crate. "What's this?"

"Eggplant. Have you never eaten one?"

"Not that I'm aware." Shaking his head, he stacked those crates, too. "I'm fairly sure I'd know if I ate anything so purple."

"Dad loved a recipe I found on the internet. Eggplant Parmesan. Baked, sliced eggplant with bread crumbs and Parmesan cheese, served on diced, cooked tomatoes." She kissed the tips of her gloved fingers. "*¡Fantastico!* I'd offer to fix it for you and let you decide for yourself, but you'd refuse to eat with me like you did last night," she said, striding away to get more vegetables.

Adam eyed her stiff, slender back and fielded a sharp stab of guilt. In truth he'd turned down her invitation for a variety of reasons; not all of them made sense today. He jumped off the truck and helped her collect more crates from the ends of the rows.

"I should have stuck around to have dinner with you last night," he said, not looking at her as he set several crates on the truck. "If I'd stayed I probably would have missed the jokers who rearranged my face. But you looked tired last night. And it had been an eventful day. Plus I knew you'd put in a long one. I didn't want you to go to the extra trouble of feeding me, Molly."

She halted beside him. "I thought maybe you turned me down because—" She broke off and hurriedly grabbed a crate of banded lettuce. "Never mind," she muttered.

"Because why?"

"Okay," she said, setting her hands on her hips. "I wondered if you thought it was improper of me to ask. I mean, you work for me, and I do live alone. It was a simple invitation. I hope you weren't worried that I'd hit on you. But if you were concerned about causing me extra work, I'm glad you told me and cleared the air."

Adam blushed. "Whenever you decide to cook those purple things next, if you invite me to dinner, I promise I won't say no."

"Really? Because once we started talking about eggplant I started to get hungry for eggplant Parmesan. If they don't all sell today I was thinking about nabbing two or three for myself. I'll be putting a casserole in the oven around seven tonight. It cooks in about thirty minutes and is a perfect side for the steak you missed last night."

"Sold," he said with a grin. "Can't we pick more if these are all sold?"

She shook her head and squinted up at him. "These would have been all the ripe ones. I don't plant a lot. Last year I noticed the locals didn't rush to buy eggplant. I suppose you're not the only one who didn't grow up with it."

He nodded. Their talk fell off. Adam hoped there would be some eggplant left. He dwelled on that alien thought for quite a while. A loner by nature, something even Jenny complained about, the eagerness he felt over the prospect of having dinner with Molly McNair seemed out of place to him.

The truck bed steadily filled up.

Finally, Molly declared them ready to wind down for the day, and she went to the barn to pay the women, taking Nitro along as she'd done the previous day.

Adam stayed behind to lash down the crates with bungee cords. When he finished he trekked to the barn. Poking his head into the office, he said, "I'm going to see how Henry's coming along flushing out the radiator on that old tractor. Holler when you're ready to go."

Acknowledging him with a short bob of her head, Molly continued to count out cash for Carlotta. "Henry usually stocks the truck with food and water for Nitro and water for us. Do you mind asking if he took care of that?"

"I'll do it if he hasn't. I know where everything is."

In another part of her mind Molly mulled over how nice it was that Adam willingly pitched in with mundane chores she'd always had to ask her other drivers repeatedly to help with. It surprised her when the ever-quiet Luisa put the same thought into words.

"He's a nice man. I hope you hang on to him, Molly. I remember how Danny Ortega and even Ramon tried to wiggle out of doing those kinds of tasks."

Glancing up, a bit flustered to know other workers had noticed such things, Molly felt it best to move on to paying Gena and passing on Luisa's remark.

The crew had all left and Molly had

locked the time sheets in the safe when Adam wandered back.

"I restocked the truck. Henry is making headway putting the tractor back together. He's working near the back door and would like us to close up in front and put out a note saying to come around back if anyone needs him."

"Can do." She took a blank sheet of paper out of the printer and wrote a quick note. "There, I'm ready if you are." She whistled and Nitro loped into the office. He stopped beside Adam until he got a head scratch, then he trotted up to Molly.

"You go on and load him in the truck. I'll bolt the door and tape on the note." She reached for the tape gun and pulled off two generous strips.

In a very few minutes they were under way. Adam pulled through the entry gate, hit the remote and waited to head for the highway until after the gate fully closed. "I'll let you program the GPS." He handed her his phone. "How many stops today?"

"Three more than yesterday." She bent over his phone. "Weekend and Wednesday markets are busiest, although some get traffic seven days a week."

"Henry didn't ask me to work weekends. I'm afraid I told my friend I'd help out in his bar on Friday and Saturday afternoons and evenings."

"I told you before, I've always handled weekends. You might not believe how much I can pack in the SUV when it's only Nitro and me."

"Okay. You said Thursday is the next time the schoolkids come to the gardens, right?"

"This year. Next school year I may add additional classes."

He said nothing. They'd entered the first town.

At the first three markets, the women who ran Molly's booths had already heard about Adam. All were solicitous toward his black eye. And everyone knew he'd saved a boy's life.

At the next stop, after they'd unloaded crates, Molly had started back to the SUV when someone ran up behind her, cupped her hands over Molly's eyes and shouted,

"Boo!" It was Tess, who laughed heartily over how far Molly jumped.

Adam observed the incident from a few feet away with a smile he wiped away the minute Molly dragged the woman over to meet him. He prepared for more gushing over saving the kid at the river.

"This is Tess Warner. Tess, Adam Hollister, my new driver. Tess has heard all about you," Molly added for his benefit.

For her part Tess gave him a lengthy once-over twice. "Nice," she murmured. "But who rearranged your pretty face?" she asked without the empathy expressed by the other women.

"I've no idea," Adam said, backing away. "Molly, I'll let you explain. I'm going to go buy eggplant. I gave them the last box. In spite of what you said about them rarely selling out, they're going fast."

"A man who likes eggplant?" Tess inquired of Molly, loud enough for Adam to hear.

"He's never had it," Molly said, then could have bitten her tongue when she added, "I volunteered to bake eggplant Parmesan for him to try."

In true Tess fashion, she tried to pin Molly down as to whether that meant Adam was joining her for dinner.

Molly didn't take the bait. "I bet your customers are glad to have you back from visiting your family," she said.

Tess nodded, all the while watching Adam pay for his purchase, which he took straight to the truck. "I see what you meant about Nitro falling for the guy. Have you staked your claim? You'd better," she advised, "or expect your territory to be poached."

Uh-oh, you might as well forget Adam if Tess, who is gorgeous and the best cook, is interested.

"I don't think Nitro's in danger of being poached," she said, meaning to be obtuse. "Listen, Tess, it's already seventy-five out and we have two more stops."

"Expect me to call and give you the third degree," Tess warned even as Molly walked away.

Buckled in her seat belt again, Molly waited for Adam to ask questions about her attractive friend. He didn't, which didn't stop Molly from putting her own spin on his opinion.

After she'd been unceremoniously dumped by Dr. Mark Lane in Africa, who Molly had thought had a prominent role in her future, she was wary of introducing a man she found attractive to friends.

She recalled how she'd introduced Mark to Penelope Volker. Penny had moved into Mark's clinic and laid claim to him posthaste.

Not that there was any comparison between Mark and Adam.

She and Dr. Lane had shared many dinners and had discussed long-term plans while walking hand-in-hand under a huge, golden, jungle moon.

Tonight would be her first informal meal with Adam—providing he didn't back out again.

And she had no claim on him at all. So there was no reason for her to have felt irritated by Tess. Her friend would make some man a better wife than Molly ever would.

Wow, is that a stretch—to leap from one

simple evening meal on your patio to wedding bells.

"You're awfully quiet," Adam said, slanting a one-eyed inspection at the woman with whom he shared a wide, bench seat. They'd left the markets for the day and Nitro snored between them. "Are you worried that our guys in the black SUV haven't showed up? Or are you concerned they still might?"

"You know, it's odd no one has ever accosted me at the markets. But I was thinking how hot it is for spring. I hope Rick got my note to irrigate the squash we transplanted."

"Do you have more plants to bring out of the greenhouse this afternoon? If so, I'll be happy to help. It's the least I can do in exchange for my first experience eating baked eggplant."

"So you're sticking by your decision to try it?"

"Did you expect me not to?"

"I didn't know. What do I really know about you?" she asked, tilting her head to one side. "You aren't exactly an open book."

"You think I have a shady past?"

"Do you?" she shot back.

He studied her for a long time when he should have been watching the highway. The silence lengthened until it felt uncomfortable in the confined interior of the cab.

He pulled down her lane and after he punched the gate opener, as they sat watching it slowly roll open, Adam cleared his throat and drummed his thumbs on the steering wheel.

"Not shady, but I've kept secrets. I was married and had a daughter. Almost two years ago my wife and child died in an accident on an icy Colorado road. An eighteen-wheeler they were following jackknifed."

Molly's mouth dropped open but she didn't know what to say.

"I should have been there, but wasn't," he said slowly. "It's not history a person lists on a job application."

Stepping on the gas, he guided the big Ford through the gate and braked on the other side until it closed.

Molly knew she was guilty of gaping. There didn't seem to be anything she could do to close her mouth. Of all the scenarios she'd conjured up about Adam Hollister, none came close to his painful truth. Sorry was such a worn-out word that it stuck in her throat now.

She hadn't known him then or his family. But she was no stranger to death. In Africa, death was no respecter of persons. She understood the agony that haunted such an intimate loss.

Rather than offer meaningless platitudes, she reached across her softly snoring dog and squeezed Adam's rigid forearm.

Briefly their eyes met. For a moment each seemed reluctant to look away. Then the moment evaporated.

Adam downshifted and drove toward the barn. The engine rumbled and Molly's hand slid away. But she knew something profound had altered the dynamics in their boss-employee relationship.

CHAPTER SEVEN

MOLLY WANTED TO SYMPATHIZE, but she couldn't find the words and so let Adam drive on to the barn in silence.

He parked, got out and began to unload empty crates.

The time passed when it would have been appropriate for her to comment on his sad situation. Her mind whirled and her heart remained heavy for him, making it take longer than usual for her to get herself and Nitro out of the cab. "I'm going to finish weeding the cabbage patch," she said into the silence.

Adam glanced up.

"I think you know your daily routine now. The way I worked with Danny, and later with Ramon, every morning I posted a list on the office window of markets and the vegetables scheduled for picking and transporting. We'll start that system tomorrow.

The rest of this week I'll organize my chores so I'll be in the office or a nearby field in case you have questions. Once you're comfortable, I won't be so handy, because I have things to do in all corners of the garden."

"Hold up. Let me finish here and I'll go with you to weed the rest of the cabbage rows. Are you going by horseback again?"

She stopped at the barn door and faced him. "Your shift is over for today. You've logged your hours and you can go home now."

Dropping a last load of blue crates, he straightened. "Have you taken back your dinner invitation? Rather than drive home and back later, I figured I'd stay and help like I did yesterday. No cost to you." Reaching back inside the truck cab, he brought out the sack of eggplant he'd bought.

She took the sack he held out. It had fled her mind that she'd promised to bake eggplant Parmesan for him. The unexpected story he'd dropped on her had stalled her brain.

"It's, uh, still…not necessary to give me free time. I'll serve dinner around seven-thirty. We can eat on the patio. When you come back, go around the house and in the side gate."

He frowned. "Okay. I don't want to be pushy. But I also promised Henry I'd see how he made out after flushing the tractor radiator. If he got it running he said I'd find him plowing the field beyond the cabbage patch. I can hike down there."

"Henry shouldn't be plowing. He's only supposed to oversee the outdoor work. He had a heart bypass while my dad was at his sickest. It's the main reason I sold all of the cattle at once. Dad expected Henry to retire. He claimed he wasn't ready to be put out to pasture and begged me to keep him on at the ranch. My dad made me swear I wouldn't let him overdo. He saved Dad's life once. Oh, I'm blathering. This is more than you probably want to know. Please take a horse and ride out to check on him. Feel free to tell him he's in for a lecture from me."

"Shall I ride Ranger again, or one of the two horses we didn't exercise yesterday?"

"It'd be great if you take Merlin. He's the sorrel quarter horse in the stall across from

Ranger. I'll ride Gigi, the paint mare. Just a warning about Merlin. He tends to eat any green plant he sees. Some vegetable leaves are toxic. Hurry him through the planted acres. Take care where you stake him out."

"Thanks for the heads-up. I had no idea anything but oleander was dangerous for animals. And I only know that because I saw it on the news."

"We don't have any on the property."

"Okay, I'll go lock the truck and hang the keys on the peg." Adam went back to take care of locking up as he spoke and before he joined Molly, who bent to unsnap Nitro's leash. The dog dashed ahead, into the interior.

She crossed in front of Adam and went into the office, and saw she still had pay slips for two days to enter in the computer. Until recently she'd been judicious about keeping abreast of paperwork. Quarterly taxes were due at the end of the week. She sat and began to enter the data.

It wasn't long before Adam led Merlin out from the area of stalls. Making a slight detour, he stuck his head in the office. "I didn't saddle the mare for you. I wasn't sure how long you'd be."

"That's fine. I'll be a while. Please go check on Henry. I really thought he was only tinkering with the tractor. I had no idea he planned to plow a field." Molly moved the bag holding the eggplant and dragged a hand through her short hair. She saw the horse dance a little, straining at the reins Adam held. "Merlin's anxious to be under way."

"Are you okay?" Adam gazed at her somewhat hesitantly.

"I'm fine." But Molly felt scattered and couldn't say why. Other than maybe she felt the pressures of the farm building up. Had she expanded too quickly? More than once Henry had said he thought she was stretching herself too thin. Was that why he took on plowing even though he knew good and well his doctor advised him to slow down?

Nitro trotted out from the back, sat at Adam's feet and butted his nose against the side of his leg.

Sparing a second to pet the dog, Adam said, "Stay, boy. Molly will take you out."

"I'll do it shortly," she said, rallying. "I can update these files after dinner." So saying, she turned off the light, slipped past Adam and closed the office door.

Taking the hint, he left the building.

Molly heard the creak of leather followed by the clip-clop of Merlin's hooves.

Whining in his throat, Nitro paced and acted for all the world as if he wanted to go with Adam. "Okay, okay. Let me fetch Gigi."

The mare, too, understood being saddled meant leaving the confines of her stall. She crow-hopped in place and tugged on the reins once Molly set the bit.

Molly made a mental note to turn all four horses out into the pasture. She needed to see if she could find the budget to hire someone to exercise them.

In the beginning she hadn't worried about money. But launching the gardens hadn't been cheap. She'd blown through her savings and now whittled away at funds left by her dad, the sale of his cattle and his insurance money. The farm had to start turning a profit soon. But where else to cut back?

She'd already taken on as many chores as she could handle.

She led Gigi out and tied her to the hitching post while she closed and locked the barn. Once saddled up she went back to musing about how she'd hate to raise her prices. Her customers had to count every penny. Molly had known that going into business, but unexpected costs such as re-orders of sprinkler heads threatened to wipe out her slim profits this month.

Plainly it was time to crunch numbers again.

Maybe she shouldn't have replaced Ramon. She'd rather not drive the big truck but that didn't mean she couldn't do it.

Of course that meant letting Adam go. Her mind blanked right there.

She loosened her hold on the reins and straightened Nitro's running line. Gigi reared. Plainly she wasn't as amenable to having the sling of hoes bumping against her as Cappy had been. Molly stopped to adjust the sling, which tightened Nitro's lead rope. Twice he barked to let her know he didn't appreciate being yanked around. "Hold on, hold on. I'm trying to fix things."

All at once the dog's body stiffened and he began to growl. Finally, Molly adjusted the sling, held the reins then spared a moment to check on Nitro. At first she thought he might be growling at a butterfly. But it settled out of sight into a flower on a potato plant. The dog's tense body grew more rigid and his growl more pronounced.

Scanning the garden, Molly caught sight of a vehicle parked a distance up the highway. Nitro's eyesight was better than hers, because that was what claimed his attention. It wasn't a car or pickup, but an ATV. She didn't see the operator. Thinking the rider might have come down the slope onto her land like that oil rep had, she perused the area again. Then the rider, who must have been bent over inspecting his back wheel, sat up. He, or she, wore a helmet, disguising the gender.

"Look, Nitro. We got all hyper for nothing. The person's leaving. Not everyone means us harm." Indeed, the ATV motored off and disappeared from view almost before the engine noise reached Molly.

Nitro did relax, and since Gigi had seemed to make peace with the sling bumping her side, Molly set off along the path.

Once settled at the cabbage patch, she could hear the tractor, but an arroyo filled with mesquite and other scrub brush choked off her view from that plot of ground. Because they acted as flood control during the rainy season when the Rio Grande often overflowed its banks, she'd left natural washes running through her property in several spots. There were sporadic places to cross, so it wouldn't be impossible to go see what Henry was doing. And it would take time away from weeding. She trusted Adam wouldn't let the older man overdo.

As she'd done the previous day, she attached her earbuds to her iPod and began to hoe in time to the best of Rascal Flatts. An hour went by before she took a break. She poured water for Nitro and Gigi, and gave the horse an apple she'd brought along. Nitro got a dog bone to gnaw on. He promptly took it to the shade.

Nearly finished another row, Molly suddenly felt as though she was being watched. She straightened, leaned on her hoe and casually shut off the music from Garth Brooks playing in her ears. Detaching one earbud, she pretended to take a water break. As she raised the bottle, goose bumps marched up her arms.

Nitro had picked up on something, too. He was on his feet, his ears pointed on full alert. A warning growl had Molly stepping across rows to reach him. Nothing moved that she could see. There wasn't even a breeze.

She no longer heard the tractor. The sun dipped into the west, indicating she'd worked longer during this stretch than she'd thought.

All at once a horse and rider materialized out of the arroyo. He was still too far away for Molly to hear hoof beats, but she recognized Merlin. Her heart beat faster. She'd been anxious over nothing. Adam must have been watching her from a distant thicket.

Although why would he?

"It's Adam," she murmured to Nitro,

whose attention remained fixed in the opposite direction even after Adam cantered
up and stopped beside her. Only then did
the Dobie look around before going right
back on point.

Molly shaded her eyes, squinting at
Adam. He had dirt on his face, no doubt
from dust kicked up by the tractor. When
he removed his sunglasses she saw the blue
bruise near his eye starting to turn yellow
and green.

"Are you knocking off for the day? I finished the plowing Henry started. He insisted
on driving the tractor back home. I would've
gone along, but he badgered me to check
on you. He showed me where to cross the
ravine. Hey, what's up with Nitro?" Adam
loosened the reins and leaned a forearm on
the saddle horn.

Not only didn't the dog greet Adam with
his usual happy wiggle, he continued to
stare downhill toward the river and growl.
It was plain from the way he tugged against
his leash that he wanted to be free to investigate.

"How long were you in the arroyo watching me work?"

Adam sat straighter. The move tightened his grip on Merlin, making the horse whicker and sidestep in a half circle. Even Gigi reacted, snorting nervously and tugging on the line that tied her to a mesquite tree.

"I don't know what you mean. I rode through the ravine without stopping. I didn't even see you until I was well down a cabbage row. I thought maybe you'd already left. What's up? Did you see someone watching you?" He forced Merlin to stay still as he scanned uphill and down.

Molly cast a sidelong glance at the dog who remained tense and focused on something unseen. "I got a creepy feeling." She shrugged. "And look at Nitro." Hands on hips, she studied the area that sloped to the river.

Adam murmured, "I believe I'll ride down along the brushy area that's claiming Nitro's attention."

"Maybe you shouldn't. Let's head home now. It's time I start dinner anyway." Molly quickly stepped over and tightened Gigi's cinch.

"You go on," Adam said. "I'll catch up."

She stopped packing the hoes in the sling. "I'll wait."

Adam touched his heels to the gelding's sides, but kept him at a slow walk.

Holding her breath, Molly slid a hand through Nitro's collar. Plainly he wanted to follow Adam. When he'd gone quite a ways and nothing had jumped out at him, she breathed again, and told herself she was letting herself get spooked over nothing.

Then Adam stopped, leaned to the right and dismounted. Before Molly had time to grow anxious again, he hailed her. "Molly, come down here, please. Don't bring Nitro."

What in the world? She tightened the loop holding the antsy dog to the tree and took off at a fast jog. Reaching Adam she saw at once why he'd summoned her. A frightened woman huddled in the thicket, tightly gripping two big-eyed children. One a toddler, the other a girl who was probably five or six.

"I think they don't understand English,"

Adam said. "Or maybe my banged-up face scared them."

Molly knelt, smiled at the family and assured them in Spanish that no one was going to harm them.

Loosening her death grip on the older child, the woman admitted in rapid-fire Spanish that she'd paid someone to bring them across the river.

"He promised to take us to Aguilares where my husband and brother are working on a ranch. He saw you in your garden and ordered us to hide. Then we came upon another man hiding here, watching you. Both men ran off. I have no more money," she cried. "He took it all, and our food and water. I'm very afraid."

Huge tears tracked down her face. Clinging to the youngest child, the sobbing woman clutched a soft-sided, bulging satchel that Molly assumed held all of their worldly possessions.

She shot Adam a furtive glance then took out her cell phone and punched in a number.

"What did she say?" he asked. "Is she ill? What's she doing here? I heard her say 'agua.' That's water, right? Are they thirsty?"

Adam dug in his saddlebag and pulled out an unopened bottle of water.

"It's not cold, but it's wet." He offered it to the woman, who took it and immediately removed the cap and gave the bottle to her oldest child, who drank without blinking or taking her eyes off Adam.

His generosity touched Molly. She'd been worried about what he'd think when she phoned someone to help the family.

The worry descended again when Adam hovered over her, asking harshly, "Who are you calling? Are you turning them in?"

"I'm calling one of my workers." Her contact answered and Molly lowered her voice. "Gena, it's Molly. I've got a mom and two kids near the river who need help...by my cabbage patch."

Speaking partly in Spanish and partly in English—eyeing Adam with trepidation—she directed Gena to take the lower river road to reach them.

Her trepidation vanished when he caught

her elbow and murmured, "Good, so you aren't calling ICE."

The woman now sharing the water with the toddler, cried out, "No, no ICE." She broke down totally and her older child flung her thin arms around her mother and sibling.

Molly glared at Adam. Dropping to her knees, she spoke softly to the woman in Spanish, assuring her she'd called for someone to take her to Aguilares.

"I didn't think they spoke English."

"Everyone in Latin America grows up knowing and fearing the acronym for Immigration and Customs Enforcement."

"Sorry. The little girl…her eyes…she's terrified. Tell them I'd never hurt them." He stripped off his headband and raked a hand through his disheveled hair.

Studying him, Molly tried to fit the few pieces she knew of him together. He was at once hard yet soft. He'd suffered tragedy. He was well spoken, well traveled, apparently, yet a professed drifter. Maybe he had worked for the government as Henry suspected. Certainly he was a puzzle not easily assembled. Turning, she delivered his message.

"Her name is Baltasar. Her husband is Joaquin." Molly might have given Adam more information on the stranded family, but their attention was diverted by a rooster tail of dust kicked up in the wake of an approaching minivan. The family tucked into the thicket couldn't see it.

"It's Gena," Molly said, her shoulders relaxing. "Her family is one of several in the area that facilitates crossings. I try not to get involved. But in this case…" Her sentence trailed off.

"In this case you did, but you're torn," Adam said. "Is that because of me?"

"Partly. You know what Deputy Powell thinks about me. Really, I don't like breaking the law."

"You didn't bring this family into the country, or steal their money and abandon them miles from their destination."

"No, but the law doesn't parse words. Everyone living on the border has the number for Border Patrol. Instead of calling them,

I phoned Gena Munoz. That puts her and us at risk."

Gena flew out of her van. She didn't look happy to see Adam standing beside Molly. "Is this a good idea?" she asked in Spanish.

"Necessary. You raised a lot of dust getting here. Shall we cut some cabbage to fill the boxes I see you have in the back of your van?"

The woman nodded. She clicked a remote and the back hatch went up.

Adam hurried over and took out three boxes. "I have a knife in my saddlebag. Do I cut the head off at the base?" he asked.

"I'll do it." Molly took two boxes from him. "You brought blankets?" she asked her friend.

"I did. You cut cabbage. Let Adam load them. I passed two BP cars on the river road. I hope they're gone by the time I go back. If not it'll be good to let them see cabbage in the back windows. I hate to take your produce, but can you fill the boxes really full?"

"Will do." Molly held her hand out for Adam's knife. "We don't want to look like we're reconnoitering here. Will you ride back up to Gigi? While you're there, settle Nitro. His barking could bring the Border Patrol."

Adam didn't argue or ask questions. He smiled at the family Gena brought out of hiding and swung into his saddle to do as Molly asked.

By the time he returned, she had the boxes filled above their tops. He carried them down the hill and set them in the cargo area so that cabbages were visible from the back window and on both sides. At a glance, from a distance, it looked as if cabbage was all Gena was transporting.

Molly didn't wait around to see her friend drive off. She untied Gigi and Nitro, mounted and galloped toward the ranch. The sling with the hoes banged against Gigi's side. She snorted and half reared.

"Hey, wait up," Adam called. He urged Merlin into a canter. "What's the rush?" he asked, catching up. His horse, too, shook his head and blew noisily through his nose. Nitro's tongue hung out from the run.

Molly glanced at Adam. "You're probably thinking I'm an old hand at what we did back there."

"I figured it happens often since your garden butts up to the river."

"You're wrong. Including today I can count on one hand the number of times I've facilitated a border crosser. All four have been women with young children. All were dumped by coyotes who robbed them blind. And all had family already living here."

"Wow, I guess that surprises me, given how many of your employees speak only a smattering of English."

She shook her head, annoyed. "I support reform. I think people should be allowed work permits, because a majority of the folks who rail against immigrants would never take the jobs they fill. But I still wish you hadn't been there today."

He reined in tight, and frowned. "Why?"

"If you tell Deputy Powell, you could torpedo my efforts here. He and his buddies will hound me and make my life miserable."

"Seems to me I aided and abetted you today." Adam sounded hurt.

She shot him a glance. "You did. Now it's my turn to ask why."

"Honestly. It was the little girl's eyes. No joy. No expectations. Maybe joining her dad will provide the sparkle she deserves."

Molly let his comment fly away on the wind as she took off at a gallop again, Adam right with her. The man was deeper than she'd thought. It made her wonder more about the family he said he'd lost. Her first impression—that kids annoyed him—had been so wrong. In fact seeing children must cause him sorrow.

At the barn, she dismounted and sped off to unlock the door.

"I'll unsaddle the horses and brush them down if you want to start supper. That's if you haven't changed your mind," he said hesitantly.

"I haven't if you're still game to try eggplant. After you feed the horses, will you turn them into the field behind the barn?"

"Sure. Hey, you said we'd eat on the patio, but I didn't see one the other day."

"It's outside the kitchen. I hope the gas

grill works. I haven't fired it up since…
well…since my dad got too sick to eat."

"Let me check it out. Frank's bar has an
indoor gas grill, so I'm pretty experienced.
I'm sure I can start it without blowing us
up." He grinned and that broke the tension
that had been between them since the encounter with the Mexican family.

"That's reassuring." Returning his smile,
Molly unhooked the sling of hoes and hung
them back on the tool rack. "See you in a
bit. I'll take Nitro with me."

Molly was surprised to find her spirits
had lifted and she looked forward to sharing her evening meal.

A while later she glanced out the kitchen
window to see Adam on the patio, fiddling
with the built-in gas grill. She felt a rush of
warmth that stole over her. And her heartbeat quickened, surprising her. But the way
his work shirt tightened across his back as
he so easily managed to get flame flickering
under the grate left her mouth dry.

In many ways Adam Hollister might be
an enigma, but he was all man.

It had been a few years since a man spoke

to the closely guarded woman in her. Spoke so loudly that for a few moments she missed the ding of the microwave that announced her two steaks were thawed.

She shook off the uncharacteristic thoughts, grabbed the steak plate and almost got bowled over by Nitro, who beat her out the back door. The dog jumped joyously around their guest. Molly rolled her eyes. "Are you as good with cooking on the grill as you are with breathing fire into it?" she asked Adam around a little laugh.

"Tell me you like medium rare and I'm your chief cook."

"Better underdone than overdone." She handed him the plate and meat fork. "I'll set the table out here. Nitro, for heaven's sake, settle down." The dog dropped to his belly and slunk over to her. Unable to resist, she scratched behind his ears. "Now look, I have to wash again, you silly dog."

Just before the screen door shut behind her, Molly heard Adam say, "It's okay, Nitro. Calm down and make her happy and I'll save you a bite of steak."

Inside, she indulged a big grin. This promised to be a better evening than she'd had in quite a while.

Table set, salad and iced tea out, Molly lit the citronella torches placed around the patio to ward off flying bugs. In the balmy night air, cicadas sang in the trees her father had planted years ago.

"The steaks are about perfect," Adam called. "How's that special dish of yours coming?"

"I just heard the oven timer go off. Choose your seat and I'll bring it out."

"This is a treat," Adam said, springing from the wrought-iron chair he'd taken to hold open the screen door for Molly who carried a hot dish between oven mitts.

"Where's Nitro?"

"He's waiting under my chair. I promised him steak."

Molly laughed. "I heard you. Think he understood?" she asked, bending to place the sizzling dish in the middle of the table.

"Are you saying you don't talk to him?" Adam pulled out her chair and waited for her to sit.

"I do. But I also sometimes talk to inanimate objects. Comes from living alone." She set the mitts aside. "I'm not used to having a gentleman around. Thank you, sir." She slanted him a smile as she sat.

"I had a single mom. She drilled good manners into me before she died." Adam returned to the chair across from her.

"We have a lot in common. I lost my mom early and was raised by my dad. What happened to your dad, if you don't mind me asking?" She passed him the salad.

"He died six months before I was born. He was an Army colonel. My mom thought he was out of Vietnam for good, but they sent him back... Stepped on a land mine."

"I'm sorry," she said.

"I've always wondered if it was one of ours. If my mother knew, she never said."

Molly was at a loss and for a moment neither of them spoke.

Finally, Adam helped himself to salad and dressing, abruptly changing the topic. "Is everything in this salad from your gardens?"

"Of course. And here's the eggplant dish. Ta-da!"

Adam took a generous helping. "It looks good." He took a bite.

Molly watched him and was pleased when he really liked it. She wanted to ask more questions about his life, but didn't find an opening.

Between bites he managed to talk about her gardens and her future plans for expansion. She could always talk about her gardens and it was nice to have someone interested in her work. Nice to have someone to talk to, period.

Dinner ended too soon.

"Would you like coffee? Or I set out a bottle of Cabernet," she said, standing to begin collecting their plates.

Adam straightened from feeding Nitro the last of his steak. "Either, unless it's too much trouble. This meal was the best I've had in a long time, Molly. Thanks. Let me help clear the table." He picked up the salad bowl and the empty steak plate.

"You don't need to help. I'll bring out the wine."

He followed her inside anyway. "Big kitchen," he said, glancing around. "Mine consists of a two-burner stove and a micro-wave."

Molly got out a corkscrew.

Adam took it and opened the bottle while she set down two wineglasses.

She watched him pour as she prepared coffee for later and tried to view her kitchen through his eyes. "Do you take cream or sugar?" she asked.

He glanced around at her. "Black, please." Adam elbowed open the screen to let her pass. They'd just taken their seats and lifted their glasses of wine when a raucous vehicle engine drowned out the singing cicadas.

Nitro bolted out from under Adam's chair, alternately snarling and barking as he raced toward the gate.

Exploding from his seat, Adam bumped the table, spilling wine everywhere as he raced after the dog.

"Don't let Nitro out," she yelled. But it was too late. Man and dog left the yard through the swinging gate.

Fearful without knowing why, Molly took another minute to dash through the house. She went out the front door and, aided by light from inside the house, was shocked to see someone on an ATV tearing across the children's garden.

More horrifying, she saw Adam close the gap between him and the roaring machine. He appeared to be gaining until Nitro streaked in front of him. The driver of the ATV kicked out at the dog then quickly turned the machine. Molly heard Nitro yelp. In the dim light cast from the porch, she saw her pet sail through the air and land hard on the ground.

Although Adam may have been able to grab the rider, he skidded to a halt and pivoted toward the now crying dog.

Molly ran from the shelter of the house, sobbing. The ATV faded into the dark, roaring up the slope to the highway where earlier Molly had observed another ATV.

"Get your SUV," Adam called. "Nitro's hip is cut. It looks pretty bad." He stripped off his shirt and wrapped the dog.

Molly bobbed her head. "I'll meet you at the car." She locked the house on shaking legs that threatened to give out.

Settled into the confines of the SUV, neither of them spoke again or ventured who or why someone was bent on destroying a simple patch of vegetables.

Battling tears, Molly concentrated on driving while Adam stemmed the flow of blood oozing from her dog's hip.

CHAPTER EIGHT

"How much farther to the vet?" Adam asked.

"Not far. How's Nitro? He seems awfully quiet." Molly slanted an anxious look at the dog.

"He's licking my hand. I triple folded the sleeve of my shirt over his wound. Maybe the extra pressure has staunched the pain and blood flow. Who would've thought he'd leap at an ATV?"

"He's a guard dog. He went after the driver."

"Unfortunately the back fender caught him when the jerk wheeled around so fast. Do you know what time it is?"

Molly checked the dash clock. "Around ten."

"Will your vet be in his office this late?"

"Harlan Talbot lives behind his clinic. At night you push a buzzer by the clinic door.

It rings in his house. If he's out he posts a phone number of a vet on call."

She glanced over at Adam, who was staring down at Nitro.

"There's his clinic. The lights are all on and there's a car out front. Maybe he's got another emergency."

Molly pulled in next to a Buick that had a large, open animal kennel in the backseat.

"He might be treating another big dog," she said distractedly. "Wait, Adam. I'll come around and open your door so you don't have to jostle Nitro too much."

Nodding, he murmured to the dog. After Molly opened the door and he stepped to the ground, Nitro buried his head in the crook of Adam's arm.

"He comes here for shots," Molly explained. "And I brought him here for neutering. Nitro's not fond of this clinic or Dr. Talbot." She tried the front door and found it unlocked. She shoved it open, setting off a loud chime.

"Have a seat. I'll be with you as quick as I can," called a disembodied voice from down a well-lit hall. Farther away dogs barked, interspersed with a few yowling cats.

Nitro began to whimper.

Adam sat in one of the plastic chairs and Molly eventually stopped pacing and dropped down on a bench. She leaned over to kiss Nitro between his ears, but realized belatedly that the move put her nose an inch away from Adam's bare chest. So she stood fast again. "You've totally ruined your shirt. I have a jacket in the car, but it'll be too small for you."

"No fret, Molly."

"Well, you can't ride home on your motorcycle without a shirt. When we get back to the ranch I'm sure there are still T-shirts that belonged to my dad that will fit you. Nitro will be okay, won't he?" she asked, switching subjects.

"I hope so. I'm more worried about having left your place without anyone around. What if that idiot returns while we're gone? Should you call the police? Or ask Henry to go over there? Just to have someone on hand?"

"Do you think the ATVer will go back?

At Henry's age he'd be no match. I can't in good conscience ask that of him, Adam. And what can cops do without us there?"

"Nothing I guess."

The vet emerged from the examining room. "Molly, hello. What's the problem?"

Molly whirled to face him. "Nitro was hit by an ATV. He has a gash on one hip."

The doctor crossed the room. "Were you driving it?" he asked Adam as he crouched to inspect the wound.

"No, Harlan," Molly rushed to say. "Adam is an employee. It's lucky he was around to help out."

"I think he's asking because of my eye," Adam said. "I ran into a fist, not an ATV," he added with a half smile.

"Ah, I see." The vet smiled knowingly. "The blood is coagulating well. Keep the pressure on," he said, rising. "I'm almost finished with my other patient. Nitro's not in danger of bleeding out, so I'll go ahead and remove the last few prickly pear spines from the other dog's nose. I won't be but a few minutes."

Molly slumped in a chair. "I saw a guy on

an ATV before I went to the cabbage patch," she admitted.

"Where?" Adam asked.

"He was parked up on the highway. Nitro spotted him first." Absently she stroked the dog's head. "The driver didn't seem interested in us, so I figured he'd stopped to check some problem with his machine. He drove off."

She looked up at Adam.

"Do you think it was the same guy? Or maybe one of the ones who jumped you?" She heaved a big sigh. "I worry I'm being targeted."

Adam shifted the dog on his lap. Big as Nitro was, his feet draped over both sides.

"Something I didn't tell you earlier," Molly went on. "The woman we helped down by the river said a man was watching me. That's why her coyote ran off."

"Did she give you a description?"

"No. I didn't think to ask for one. I was intent on getting her help. He must've been on foot or she would've mentioned a vehicle. The two incidents probably aren't related. I'm just feeling paranoid."

"The schoolkids come again tomorrow, right?"

"Yes," she said, looking glum. "Most of the damage was to their garden."

"Are there steps we can take early in the morning to repair any of it?"

"I'll have to check when it's light. He would've done more if you and Nitro hadn't scared him off."

A tall woman carrying a sad-eyed German shepherd emerged from the examining room. "Thanks, Dr. Talbot," she said. "Oliver probably won't chase rabbits into my cactus garden again."

"You may need to put up a fence. Some dogs never learn," the doctor said, motioning for Molly and Adam to go into an adjoining room.

"I probably need to fence along the highway," Molly muttered after they entered the room. "Henry and I talked about it."

"That's a long border. It'd be costly."

"That's why I haven't done it yet. I could plant sunflowers all along there."

Dr. Talbot entered the room pulling on rubber gloves. "Now let's have a better look at this fellow." He tapped a finger on the exam table, indicating Adam should lay Nitro there. Reaching up, the doctor turned on a high-intensity light. And once Adam gently peeled away his bloody shirt, the vet directed the beam at the dog's hind quarters.

Nitro cowered and flailed his front paws. Molly quickly moved to the opposite side of the table and stroked her hand down his shaking body.

"It's deep, but it could be worse," Talbot said. "It needs subcutaneous and cutaneous closing. I'll suture with absorbable material that won't need to be removed and then use Vetbond tape rather than suture him closed. I'll need one of you to hold him tight."

"I can." Adam spoke solemnly, placing his big hand over Molly's. "Are you okay with that?"

She was grateful for the comfort transmitted through his simple touch. "I'm wobbly, but I'll help, too. I don't want to leave Nitro."

"Are you sure? You look done in."

The vet studied her. "He's right."

"I've seen worse injuries with the Peace Corps."

Talbot scrubbed up before pulling on a new pair of rubber gloves. "Since you're staying, Molly, hold his hind legs so I can cleanse the wound. Adam, you take his head and front paws."

The vet worked swiftly, but talked as he flushed out the wound. "He'll wear an Elizabethan collar for ten days to two weeks so he can't lick or scratch off the tape."

The dog let out a howl and scrabbled to escape. Molly tightened her grip.

Talbot directed Adam to hold Nitro's neck steady. "I'll sew and tape him up quickly." The doctor readied his needle and gauze pad to sponge away blood.

"So, Molly, who was riding the ATV this late at night?" the vet asked as he took tiny stitches deep in the wound.

Molly had to raise her voice because Nitro had begun to howl. "No idea. Deputy Powell thinks I ruffled some feathers by selling Dad's cattle and planting gardens."

"Hmm. What about the folks from the oil company?"

Adam's head jerked up.

Seeing him out of the corner of her eye,

Molly raised her head, too. "Oil c-company f-folks?" she stammered, shifting gears away from watching the doctor work to wondering why her vet knew about the oil guys.

Talbot set aside the needle, doused the new stitches with saline and closed the outer skin together with two lengths of tape before he glanced up again.

"Okay, Adam, lift his head." The vet fastened a wide plastic collar around the animal's sweating neck and, with an economy of motion, gave him a shot.

"That's an antibiotic. Should hold him for a couple of days. I'll write a script for pills I want him on for a week to ward off infection." He wrote one out, handed it to Molly and then said, "When I certified health on your dad's herd one day, he had a couple of testy visitors. Oil representatives, he said, who wanted to buy mineral rights to the ranch. When he said no, I gather they pressured him to let them test various sites. He told me when he refused, the pair got really belligerent. Among other things they accused him of being unpatriotic. Mike was quite ill by then. He was afraid they'd pressure you after he was gone."

"I knew about them. One paid me a visit," Molly admitted then trained her eyes on Nitro who'd begun to shake his head. "The guy gave me a business card. It didn't say who he was, but listed the oil company. I plan to look them up online. Surely a legitimate company wouldn't resort to intimidation, Harlan."

The vet shrugged. "I only brought it up because I have a veterinarian friend in the Midwest who I saw at a recent conference. He had his property confiscated through eminent domain for the tar sands pipeline. The oil men convinced the state to take his land and a whole line of small farms."

Molly gaped. "You mean the state stole land?"

"Legislators set what they called a fair price, but my friend said it amounted to pennies on the dollar for what the going rate was for his area. I've since seen on the news that in other states groups are banding together to fight similar takeovers."

"That's awful. But I haven't heard of anything like that here," Molly said.

"I shouldn't have said anything. I'm probably way off base."

Nitro whined and bumped against Adam, who spoke softly and rubbed the dog's ears. "I hope he doesn't associate me with all this pain and surgery."

"Oh, poor dog," Molly crooned.

The dog chafed at the collar.

Dr. Talbot addressed Adam. "Hold him while I ready a cage in the back." Removing his gloves, he tossed them in a metal trash can. "I expect he'll do fine. You can pick him up around noon tomorrow."

Talbot left the room.

Adam sat in one of the two chairs with Nitro on his lap. Holding him close, which wasn't easy with the collar, the man calmed him by swaying gently.

Molly took the second chair.

"I can swing by here for him tomorrow after I finish deliveries."

"My brain feels so muddled. Thanks for thinking ahead. His injury didn't look so bad once Harlan cleaned up the blood, did it? Or is that wishful thinking on my part?" she added, reaching out to touch Nitro. "It looked pretty deep."

"We're lucky it wasn't a longer gash. Still, it cut muscle. Thankfully it missed severing a tendon."

"It infuriates me to think anyone would be so senselessly mean."

"Absolutely."

A door opened and closed somewhere, followed by heavy footsteps passing their room. "I wonder if Harlan had another emergency." Molly got up, opened the door to the examination room and peered out.

She looked back at Adam as she began to close the door, only to have it jerked out of her hand. She squealed and flinched.

A young man entered the room. He beamed at her. "Sorry if I startled you. I'm Ron Davis, Dr. Talbot's intern. He has a cage ready in the hospital area for your Dobie."

He crossed to where Adam still sat. "Don't worry about his care tonight. I have night duty. Can you carry him to the cage?" he asked. "Don't mind the noise back there.

We have several vocal patients. Most are ready to go home." He scratched Nitro between his flattened ears. "I understand he's a trained guard dog."

"Well, kind of. Lately he's a big softie," Molly said. "But since he's hurt, I don't know how he'll react. Earlier he scared off an intruder. He deserves hugs."

Adam shifted Nitro to a better position. "Molly, would you grab my shirt? I don't know if it can be salvaged, but I should try."

She picked it up where it laid wadded on a chair. And she scooped up her purse from the floor before following the men out of the room. "Should I shut off the light?"

Ron turned back. "Don't bother. A cleaning crew is here in about ten minutes."

"Really? They come in at midnight?"

Adam glanced over his shoulder. "Is it that late? We'd better settle him then get out of here if we want that early start to repair the garden."

Molly agreed, but they stayed a while after Adam tucked the dog into a large, walk-in cage, setting him on the straw bed.

"I hope he can eat and drink with that collar on," Molly murmured.

Ron knelt down. "I'll help him get the hang of it. By the way, Dr. Talbot went home to fix some dinner. When I came in he said he hadn't broken for lunch. Busy day and long night, and it's not even a full moon."

"Is that true about a full moon?" Molly handed Adam his soiled shirt, although her question was aimed at Davis.

"We deliver more animal babies at that time than any other. My people-doctor friends say it's the same for humans."

Nitro got to his feet. He sniffed the bowl of water then lapped some up.

Molly watched him before the intern closed the cage. "His drinking water is a good sign. I feel better about leaving now."

"Me, too." Adam rose from where he knelt.

"Dr. Davis, you have my phone number if anything changes with his condition."

He picked up a five-by-seven-inch card from on top of the cage and rattled off a phone number. "Is that correct, Ms. McNair?"

"Yes. So I guess we can go," she said to Adam, failing to stifle a yawn.

The cacophony of animal voices faded as they left, prompting Molly to remark on the silence when they stepped out into the night. "It's so quiet. Do you think they're immune to the racket? How do they know if an animal is hurting as opposed to expressing unhappiness about being there?"

"I suppose like a parent can distinguish their child's cry of pain from simply not wanting to go to bed." He opened her driver's door then said, "Would you like me to drive?"

"Thanks, but I'm okay."

They got in and she backed around. Partway down the lane she passed a van, and watched it carefully in the rearview mirror.

"That must be their cleaning crew," Adam said, turning his whole body to check on the other vehicle.

"I forgot Ron said they were due." She rubbed a hand over her forehead. "I must be getting paranoid."

"No one could blame you." Adam rolled

down his window and let in the cool outside air.

"I wonder if I left any lights on at home."

"It wouldn't take much to put some perimeter lights on a motion detector."

"That might have confounded the ATV guy sooner and saved poor Nitro and the children's garden. Would it be hugely expensive?"

"I don't think so. Depending on your wiring, I might be able to do it."

She spared him a curious glance. "You're really a man of many talents."

He waited until she'd turned off the highway onto her ranch road then said, "Did you mean that as a compliment or not?"

Molly felt a flush slip up her neck. "Of course. As much help as you've been to me, Henry and Nitro, why would I be sarcastic?"

Adam shrugged. "You're right," he mumbled. "You're too nice to be sarcastic."

Frowning, Molly pressed the remote and let the SUV idle while the gate opened. She drummed her fingers on the steering wheel. "This gate is a farce. Anyone can get out, push the button and it opens. And intruders can come onto the property from a host of unsecured avenues."

She shifted into drive and out of habit waited on the other side until the gate rumbled shut behind her. Only then did she step on the gas and drive on, slowing dramatically as she approached the house. "Ugh, like I thought, I didn't leave a light on anywhere."

Bracing his hands on the dashboard, Adam scanned the stark outline of the barn and house. "Even the moon's dark tonight," he observed. "I don't know if they have it here, but in some towns there's an app you can get for your cell phone to turn on your lights."

"Even if it's available it could be expensive. I've burned through a lot of money getting the gardens to the point of producing. Unless I plant mature pecan and citrus trees in the area you and Henry plowed today, I won't have much of a winter crop to carry me through to spring."

"Are you saying you're running on a shoestring?"

She parked and shut off the engine but left the lights on to cast a glow around them.

"What's longer than a shoestring, but just short of enough to hang myself?" she said and laughed.

"Come on. I'll walk you to the door and check around inside. Then if you give me a key to the barn, I'll bunk there tonight."

Molly took a breath as if to object, but Adam cut in. "I saw a cot in the tack room."

"Nobody's slept there for a long time. When the ranch operated at its peak Dad had wranglers who stayed in a bunkhouse. I tore it down for a greenhouse. He also had a stableman taking care of our horses." She gazed nervously into the gloom. "The mattress on the cot is old and probably lumpy." She paused to haul in a ragged breath. "I shouldn't let you stay. But, frankly, without Nitro for company tonight…" She let out a breath. "Do you want Dad's bed for the night?"

Adam smiled. "You do ramble on," he said, opening his door as she shut off the auto lights and stepped out. "But I'm fine in the tack room." he said.

"Whoa! It's blacker than black out here," Molly said, stumbling to the front of the vehicle. "Why would I have shut out the porch light?"

"You were rattled." Adam felt his way around the grille, found her hand in the dark and clasped it. "This is as close to the blind leading the blind as I can imagine."

He pulled out his cell phone and turned on the flashlight app. The small circle of light it created didn't do much.

They moved forward in a series of baby steps. Finally, Molly said, "My eyes are adjusting." She set out more confidently for the house, but kept hold of Adam's hand.

On reaching the door, even with the phone light, it took a several stabs with her key to hit the lock. "This will teach me to always leave a light on if I'm going out at night."

At last the door gave under her ministrations and she was able to go inside and turn on some lights. "I'm good now," she told him. "You can let go."

"Ah, sure." Stepping inside, he pocketed his phone and listened intently as she turned on hall lights and one in the kitchen.

"Would you like that cup of coffee we

never got to drink after dinner? I can make a fresh pot."

He peered into rooms off the hall. "Late as it is, I think I'd rather hit the hay."

She hurried into the end bedroom and soon returned with her arms full. "Everything was easy to find. Here's the shirt, plus sheets, a pillow and a blanket. And let me grab you a key." She removed it from a peg in the kitchen.

Adam had held out his arms and let her pile them full. She found his hand beneath the stack and looped the key ring over his thumb.

"Thanks." He walked outside. "Don't shut out the porch light until you see I've turned one on in the barn. Say, if there's no sign of me when you emerge, give me a yell."

"Sure. I'll bring you coffee and a couple slices of toast, shall I?"

Already down the cinder walkway, he called back, "That'd be great. Sleep tight, and don't let the bedbugs bite."

"Funny man," she responded, hearing the teasing banter lacing her own words.

Yes, it makes a mountain of difference to know he'll be sleeping a stone's throw away.

It surprised her to discover she liked having their lives intertwined. And it certainly wasn't a hardship to study the sway of his body until he melted into the darkness nearer the barn. Molly didn't budge from her doorway until she saw light leak out through the door he opened.

ADAM LOCKED THE door behind him and hurried to the tack room where he dumped the bedding on the cot. Several times over the course of the evening his cell phone had vibrated. He hadn't bothered to check to see who it was, but only a few people had his cell number. It might be Frank Tully wanting to schedule him to work at the bar. But he'd never known Frank to be so persistent.

He dug the phone out of his pocket and saw that he'd missed eight calls to be exact. The last one had been ten minutes ago. The caller information was blocked. It could be a wrong number.

He set the phone on a bench, but as he made up the cot a chill swept up his spine.

The last time he'd had a persistent caller this late at night, it'd been Colorado Highway Patrol calling him in the Middle East to tell him of Jenny and Lindy's accident.

Needing to shake off the gloom, he went into the stable to wash up in the sink he'd seen there. On returning to the tack room he felt cleaner, but still disturbed. When he sat to pull off his boots, his cell rang again. He grabbed it and growled, "Hello!"

"Adam, where in blue blazes are you? I sat in Tully's until it closed, and I've been waiting on your doorstep since midnight."

"Dave?" Tucking the phone between his ear and bare shoulder, Adam let his heart settle as he toed off his second boot. He wiggled his toes and waited for his former business partner to say why he was calling. Why he'd called relentlessly over five hours.

"Have you moved? The bar owner said you still lived in the trailer."

"Asks the man who disconnected the number he gave me," Adam snapped. Silence ensued. "Dave? You still there?"

"I need to know what progress you've made finding oil on the McNair ranch."

Adam ripped off his socks and unbuckled his belt while he chose how to answer. "None. Are you aware two thugs tried to run me off the road in Ms. McNair's flatbed? The same two may have jumped me at my place—when, I might add—I'd managed to collect a sample."

Dave sucked in a quick breath but before he could say anything, Adam cut him off.

"And the two who jumped me broke that sample, which is why I've made absolutely no headway."

He thought he heard Dave groan.

"I'm fine, thanks for asking. They got in a few good licks before hightailing it. And they don't know you. What gives? Tonight a guy on an ATV popped wheelies around one of the gardens and clipped Ms. McNair's dog, sending him to the vet."

Adam got no response.

"What do you know about those incidents?" he asked, prodding.

"Nothing," Dave said sullenly. "I've got my own troubles, man. I need the finder's fee the head of Branchville promised if you locate oil on the property. I've heard they're talking to a few state legislators who are keen to add the jobs a new oil field will bring to Texas. They'll get the oil if it's there, with or without us."

"Without me! Ms. McNair runs an organic farm. If she were to let anyone sink a well or wells on her land, USDA regulators would put the kibosh on her marketing her produce."

"I've visited those markets, Adam. She can't make ends meet on what she sells. Have you told her how much she can make owning the mineral rights to two or three producing wells? She could go play princess on the Riviera."

"She isn't the type."

"Say, you aren't going mushy over her, are you, buddy? I didn't expect that from you, of all people." Dave gave a laugh that grated on Adam's nerves.

"And you, of all people, ought to know I don't approve of strong-arm tactics."

There was a definite sneer in Dave's voice when he responded. "Time's growing short for Branchville to show the federal government they have a new domestic oil site.

They can't afford to lose fifty percent of the funding. I know for a fact Branchville's head honchos are exploring ways to get the state to screw Ms. McNair out of her land. If they succeed, Adam, we get no money from the deal and she won't earn what her land is worth."

Hopping up, Adam paced the small space. He must be missing something. Granted he was beat. Then he recalled what Harlan Talbot had said about his friend in the Midwest who'd lost his property to eminent domain.

"Hello? Hello?" Dave yelled.

"I'm here," Adam snapped. "I know Molly has put her heart and soul into building these gardens on land her family has owned for generations. She'll fight them in court, Dave."

"And she'll lose. Since you sound as if you care, you'd better convince her that her gardens can coexist next to wells. Tell her to forget organic. Listen, I'll call you in a week or so. I hope you'll have talked some sense into the woman. I really hope you haven't lost your charm, pal."

"Wait! I'm not going to... Dave? Dave!"

Adam felt like throwing his phone against the wall. What hadn't Dave understood about his position? Slamming his phone down, he shucked off his jeans, turned out the light and dropped down on the cot.

Unable to fall asleep, he wondered why money was an issue. They'd both made more than any two men needed. But Dave had sounded desperate.

As he lay thinking how his savings and stocks had built and built since he'd signed the company over to Dave, Adam couldn't imagine why that wouldn't be enough cash to last any man a lifetime.

As he finally felt his limbs grow heavy, he continued to ponder how he might help Molly without letting on he'd come here for less than aboveboard reasons.

Maybe he should come clean. Would she care that he'd changed his mind?

His last coherent thought was that Dave had been right; he was going mushy over Molly McNair.

ADAM JERKED OUT of a pleasant dream to someone pounding on his door. It took him a few minutes to recall where he was. "Okay, I'm awake," he responded. "Is it light outside? It's still pitch-dark in here."

He heard Molly's melodic laugh on the other side of the door. "I've brought coffee and toast like we discussed," she called. "To be honest it's barely light. I'm anxious to see the extent of damage to the children's garden."

"Right. Give me a minute." He folded back the sheet and blanket he didn't remember crawling under. Yesterday's blood-stained pants would have to do, he thought, yanking them on in the dark.

Adam had decided to go sometime today to collect his clothes and a few things from the trailer. Unless Molly threw him out, he intended to bunk here at least until Nitro's hip healed.

After he tugged on the T-shirt she'd loaned him, he turned on a light and opened the door. "That coffee smells like heaven," he said, reaching for one of two mugs she held. He took the one with a slice of toast balanced on top.

"Did you sleep okay on that lumpy cot?"

He nodded.

"I must say I slept like the dead. While the coffee perked I phoned the clinic. I woke Ron Davis. Nitro had a good night."

"I'm glad." Adam bit into the toast and swallowed it with a slug of coffee. "Once I got to sleep I didn't wake up, as you discovered. Before we get started for the day I want to run something by you. It crossed my mind that Nitro won't be up to guard duty for a week or so. What if I bring a few things and stay here? We don't know the ATVer won't strike again," he rushed to say, because he saw her brow pucker.

He gobbled down his toast and they both did justice to their coffee before Molly finally replied. "Yes, I think I'm okay with you staying here."

Adam smiled. "Okay, then let's get to work."

CHAPTER NINE

LAVENDER AND PINK streaks had begun to layer the eastern sky when Molly and Adam set their empty coffee mugs on the office desk and left to inspect last night's damage. She pulled out gloves that poked from her back pocket and tugged them on, although she still felt a little off-kilter.

Adam Hollister had looked much too appealing when he'd stepped out of the tack room, still a bit rumpled from sleep.

She'd sworn to Tess that she didn't want or need a man in her life, but the more Molly saw of Adam, the less sure she was about that. The man had a way of sauntering that left her mouth dry as dust, she thought, watching him cross to retrieve his gloves from his bike's saddlebags.

Sucking in fresh air, she spun away and reached the garden before him. At first she walked up and down the rows, bending several times to replant limp but unbroken vegetables.

Once Adam joined her, she stood. "It's not as bad as I feared. I think he only managed two swipes across the garden."

"I see tracks where he came down, then deeper ruts where he gunned his ATV to go back up. He had no lights. I didn't see which way he went on the highway, did you?"

"No, I was too worried about Nitro. I suppose I should phone Deputy Powell and report this. Or is it too late?"

"He may come take a look. If you explain it was late and we had to get Nitro to the vet, he can't fault you for the delay. While you're on the phone, what should I do?"

She unclipped a key ring from her belt. "The squash we transplanted took the brunt of his tires. Do you remember where we got these plants in the greenhouse?"

He nodded.

"If you'll fill a couple of the wagons with flats of new starts and bring them out, between those and the carrots, peas and beans

I can salvage, possibly the kids won't realize anything happened out here."

"You're more optimistic than me," he said, taking the key. "Tell Powell we're going to replant areas that were wrecked. Maybe that will move him to drive out here quicker."

"Good thinking." She hauled out her phone and scrolled through her contacts.

Adam trekked to the greenhouses.

Molly was again reviving plants when he returned.

"Did you get Powell?"

"He's on his way. All he asked is that we don't disturb the tracks to and from the highway."

"Shall I pop plants into the vacant spots along the squash rows?

"If you don't mind. And collect the ones he destroyed. Try to smooth out the dirt along the row as best you can." She showed him how.

They worked in silence and had nearly all the rows restored when the deputy rolled in.

"I'll talk to him, Adam, if you'll take the wagon back. Toss the ruined plants in the brown Dumpster between the two green-houses. They're too dirty to compost."

Giving her a thumbs-up, he grabbed both wagon handles and took off.

Henry drove in behind Deputy Powell. After he parked at the barn, he got out and flagged down Adam. *"¿Qué pasa?"* he called out in Spanish.

Luckily it was one of few Spanish phrases Adam knew. "Walk with me to dispose of these wrecked plants."

The manager fell into step and Adam ran down the list of events from the previous evening.

"So you know, I spent the night in the tack room." He watched for Henry's reaction. "With Nitro laid up for a while, I suggested to Molly that I stick around nights until he gets better."

The older man helped toss plants into the Dumpster. "I couldn't agree more. There's already a fridge in the barn. The wife and I have an extra microwave in our garage I'll bring over. How about if I tell Molly I asked you to stay? Otherwise she might renege, especially if she thinks she's putting you out."

"I won't let that happen, trust me. Let's go see what the deputy is saying."

The men left the wagon in the greenhouse and took a more direct path back to where Molly stood talking to Deputy Powell. They arrived in time to hear Powell say, "Dispatch also reported taking an anonymous tip this morning. Someone claimed they recently saw you assist some illegals after they crossed the river."

Molly shot a glance at the two men who'd walked up.

Adam removed a glove and casually set his hand on her shoulder. "Maybe someone driving by on the river road saw me pull Bobby Parks out of the water." He focused on Powell. "Kid hit his head and almost drowned. Another boy left and fetched Bobby's mother. It might have looked to an observer as if we were helping people cross. The Parks family live in the village. You can talk to them," he said smoothly and squeezed Molly's shoulder.

"I know Eldon Parks." Powell brushed a thumb back and forth across his bottom lip. "His boys and their friends are always giving their parents grief. You say you two pulled his kid out of the river?"

"Adam did." Molly cleared her throat but didn't say when. "Several boys were swimming. They'd been told not to go without an adult."

"Look," Adam said, "here come the pickers. I'm sure some of them can verify what happened. I'll get Gena, shall I?" he said pointedly to Molly. "She said her son was shaken over his good friend's near drowning. You want to finish filling the deputy in on last night's incident while I fetch her?"

"Thanks, Adam." Eyeing Henry, she said, "Did Adam tell you what happened last night? We took Nitro to Harlan's clinic. He sewed up a deep cut."

"Adam said Nitro leaped at an ATV driver who'd driven onto the property from the highway."

"Yes, he interrupted the jerk's attempt to ruin the garden. The ATVer whipped around to leave and his back fender hit Nitro."

"He must be okay. Adam said he's picking the dog up after his market run today."

"That's the plan."

Deputy Powell had gone up the slope to study tire tracks leading to and from a section of highway where even now a few vehicles whizzed past.

Adam jumped back over the rows. Gena followed more slowly.

Molly, well aware how many of her employees, like Gena, didn't trust Border Patrol or the local police, turned to hug the uneasy woman.

"Deputy Powell tells us someone phoned an anonymous tip to his dispatcher. They insinuated I helped a river crosser. Adam thinks maybe the caller mistook his rescue of Bobby Parks."

Deputy Powell rejoined them; his features were a mask, his eyes hidden behind reflective sunglasses.

"Yes." Gena gestured with a hand. "The whole village is so grateful you two were down there hoeing weeds. Our kids are still shaken."

Powell shrugged. "Maybe they'll stay away from the river now."

"Maybe." Gena checked her watch and

cast a quick glance back at her friends who'd already set to work.

Delivering Gena another hug, Molly smiled. "If you've no more questions for Gena," she said, glancing at the deputy, "I don't want her to lose picking time. Time equals money to the workers and to me."

"Understood. All the same, if you don't object, I'll have a look around the place and inside your barn and outbuildings. I doubt even a bleeding heart like you would put border crossers up in your home, but I'd appreciate having access to it, too."

Molly narrowed her eyes.

Henry cut in before she could say anything she might regret. "I'll escort the deputy around, Molly. The greenhouse and sheds are open. I think you already unlocked the barn, didn't you?" He aimed his query at Adam.

"Yep. But remember I slept in the tack room last night."

"I'm glad you did. Molly, I want Adam to stay here nights until Nitro's fully recovered. And don't argue."

Molly's jaw tensed. "I don't like being

ganged up on, Henry. I'm going to call Tess Warner. If she's not baking bread tonight I'll ask her to bring Coco and spend the night."

Her manager scoffed. "That little porker she calls a dog would lick an intruder to death. Even if she's here, I'll feel better knowing Adam is a yell away."

Molly made a face at him.

Powell and Henry walked off, and she glanced at Adam. "It's a huge imposition, expecting you to stay. Honestly, Henry sometimes feels he has to treat me like he thinks my dad would. He forgets I'm a grown woman."

"We know you're not a kid. But don't you agree that the more vehicles parked around, the less likely somebody will try something? Henry offered to bring me a microwave. I already called Frank Tully, who I rent from. If you have a friend coming this afternoon, I'll go by my place and grab clothes to tide me over for a week or so."

"Well, if you've already made arrangements… Probably the least I should do to reciprocate is feed you. So, join me for dinner tonight even if Tess does come."

"I'll make do. You two enjoy yourselves. Ah, I see the pickers are getting way ahead of me. I'll bring the truck down and start loading."

"Did you grow up with sisters?" she asked abruptly.

He angled his head. "No siblings. I was thirteen when my mom died of a heart ailment. I, uh, was sent to live with my aunt. I left at seventeen when I got a scholarship for college."

"Adam, I'm sorry. I always seem to put my foot in my mouth around you. I'm so sorry, too, about the loss of your wife and daughter. Your admission came as such a shock I didn't know what to say at the time."

"It's not something I'm in the habit of mentioning. I-it…uh… You've also suffered losses. I wanted you to know I understand the roller-coaster feelings that can strike without warning or provocation."

"It's a terrible bond to share, but to be honest I also feel it. And you read my mind about giving Gena a heads-up on the anonymous call. Powell obviously still thinks I'm doing something to bring on all of these attacks."

"The jerk. He's intent on finding you guilty of harboring border crossers."

"We agree on that, too. Great minds and all." She gave a little laugh.

"Thanks. Now, though, I do have to get to work." He left her with a smile.

She tracked his retreat, all the while thinking she ought to tell him he should smile more often. Then again that smile, which creased his cheeks and lit his eyes, made him far too alluring. She could easily fall for him.

Before she dwelled on the notion too long, she pried her phone out of her jeans' pocket and called Tess. "Hi...it's Molly." Launching straight into her latest debacle, she wound down, saying, "If you're not scheduled to bake tonight I wondered if you might bring Coco and come for dinner and then spend the night?"

"I can, but why don't you bring Nitro and stay at my place? I mean, are we in danger if that guy decides to hit your place again?"

"You remember meeting Adam, my truck

driver? He's going to bunk in the tack room until Nitro's back to normal. Also, if my house is well lit, and there are cars around, the guy should think twice about coming back."

"Hmm. Just one question. Why doesn't the long, tall, handsome hunk of manhood bunk in the house, my friend?"

"I offered him my dad's bed last night. He turned me down. The man's not looking for a relationship. In fact it's so sad. He told me his wife and daughter died in an accident a couple of years ago. He's probably still grieving."

"Oh. I'm sorry to hear that. Sorry I jumped to the wrong conclusion."

"Listen, I got up early this morning and put stew in the Crock-Pot. Does that and a green salad suit you for dinner?"

"Anything suits me if someone else cooks." Tess laughed. "I know you make a better salad than I ever will, so I'll bring bread."

"Okay. The stew will be ready by six-thirty or seven. See you."

"This will be fun. I haven't been to a pajama party in years. I have a pair of outra-geous ones covered with neon skeletons that I've never worn."

"Don't expect me to have anything re-motely like that. Summers I wear shorts and a tank top to bed. In winter I drag out my comfy flannel pj's."

"Figures, but I'll bring my shocking ones anyway. If we have to dash out in the mid-dle of the night after an intruder, I may be what frightens him off."

The women said their goodbyes and hung up. Molly tucked her phone back in her pocket, feeling fortunate to have a gregari-ous friend like Tess.

Henry's wife, Alma, used to accuse Molly of hiding her light under a bushel. When she was younger she hadn't understood what Alma meant. Now that she did, she knew it was true.

Vowing to try to be more outgoing, she mentally checked off a list of what she needed to do next and struck out for the barn. Glancing up, she saw Henry and Dep-uty Powell heading toward her.

She changed course to meet them, as

Henry signaled her. But it was Powell who spoke. "I don't have a warrant to go inside your home. Henry's let me check everywhere else. All the men you currently have toting your irrigation pipes have no immigration issues. To clear you of the anonymous charge, I should check inside the house."

Molly stared at him a moment, wanting badly to refuse on general principle. Instead she withdrew a key from the watch pocket of her jeans and handed it to Henry.

"I guarantee the only unwanted guests you'll find in my house are an overabundance of dust bunnies. But knock yourself out."

Powell removed his shades. He looked down his nose and twirled them by one stem. "I'm quite sure your daddy would disapprove of your attitude toward the law. Mike was a gentleman through and through. You'd do well to follow his lead."

"Actually, on more than one occasion Dad suggested if I was going to do business in this community I'd need more sass and vinegar."

Henry smothered a grin.

Powell hitched up his utility belt and turned toward the house. "Let's go. I have other duties to see to."

After rolling his eyes, Henry charged after the lawman, leaving Molly standing with her hands on her hips.

Adam placed a last crate on the truck, shed his gloves and sauntered over. "Is everything all right? You look annoyed."

She dropped her arms. "I shouldn't let that man rile me so, but I can't seem to help it. He rubs me wrong."

"Why are they going into your house?"

Molly wrinkled her nose. "To make certain I'm not hiding undocumented immigrants under my bed."

"Are you kidding?"

"No. I'm irritated at myself. It's plain the anonymous tipster saw us help that woman and her children. In truth, I'm more scared over how it might have ended than angry that Powell suspects me. If the person who saw us had had a cell phone, they could have had me...us...dead to rights in a photograph." She slanted Adam a glance. "I shouldn't have let you get involved."

He gathered her wrists in a move that seemed unconscious because of the serious way he studied her face. "Wouldn't anyone with half a heart give humanitarian aid to a young mom dumped out on the desert alone with two little kids?"

Shivering at the feel of Adam's thumbs sliding along the inside of her wrists, Molly slowly shook her head. "Ranchers have a habit of looking the other way. Do you recall me saying Powell would leap on any reason to charge me under some federal statute? At least, that's the impression he gives. I'd be forced to hire a lawyer. But that's costly and it could languish in the courts for years. Of course, I could claim in court that I gave water or food to keep them from dying on my property." She took a deep breath. "Gena risked more. What she did by transporting that family is a felony. Powell would toss her in jail and still deport the mom and her kids."

"What a stupid waste of time. Still, it

won't serve you well to rile the deputy. It'll only make him watch you closer."

"You're right. A voice of reason. Thanks, Adam. He just makes me hot under the collar. It's as if he's happy to investigate my place for undocumented workers instead of hunting for whoever's harassing me."

Pulling her closer, Adam slid his arms around her back. He tucked her head under his chin and tightened his hold a fraction. "Before I leave for my route I'll ask him if he's had any luck tracing that paint on the truck to local body shops. While I'm at it I'll ask if he's aware of any ATV owners in the area. Finding who did this last night is probably futile, but if he lets it be known he's looking into the incident, the person responsible may not come back again."

Surprised by how much comfort she derived from the steady beat of Adam's heart, Molly took her time digesting his words. Finally she sighed and stepped away. "Right. But I should be the one to question Powell. Go ahead and go to market."

"Do you still want me to pick up Nitro when I'm finished?"

"Please. Unless you have other plans. I'm leaning on you more than I have any right to do."

He hesitated a moment. "I'll do whatever I can to never let you down." He took two steps back then turned and strode to the truck.

Squinting to keep the swing of his wide shoulders in sight, Molly nibbled thoughtfully on her upper lip.

What an odd thing to say.

She watched Adam vault into the flatbed where he began strapping down the stacked crates. Then Carlotta called out, "Molly, we're done for today. Shall we meet you in the office?"

"By all means." She stepped across the rows to join up with the women. Several of the pickers stopped short of the end of the rows. The roar of the Ford's motor as Adam prepared to leave interrupted one of them asking about the deputy's SUV still parked by the corral.

"I called him. Last night someone drove an ATV through the schoolkids' garden. Nitro gave chase and got hurt."

"We wondered where he was today. Is he okay?"

"He'll be laid up a few days, but Adam's going to go to the vet and fetch him later."

"I guess that's why he was hugging you. Because you feel bad, huh?"

Of course the workers had seen Adam holding her. It'd be foolish to think they'd miss something so out of character for her. The women's very active grapevine would start working overtime.

And maybe she could've read too much into his simple embrace. He was a caring man.

"Ladies, I see Henry and Deputy Powell coming our way. Henry can let you in the office and I'll only be a minute."

They complied quickly. Molly had seen how uneasy they were when Powell drove in. "Henry, I need a word with Deputy Powell." He handed her back her house key and veered off toward the barn.

"I couldn't find anything in your house," Powell said. "I presume that's what you want me to say. Henry's been assuring me all your morning workers are documented."

"Definitely. Say, I forgot to ask earlier if you'd found any trace of the black SUV that hit our truck and was in for repairs."

"Nothing. You should be receiving a copy of my report in the mail. My staff checked several vehicles matching the description Hollister gave. None showed scrapes on their right side. And since they weren't in the ditch when I arrived, their vehicle was drivable."

"I'd hoped something would turn up. Can you think of anyone in the area who owns a silver ATV?"

Powell unsnapped his shirt pocket and took out a small notebook. "Did you tell me it was silver?" He thumbed through a few sheets. "I thought you told our dispatcher it was dark out. No moon and all."

"True. But I may have seen the same ATV up on the highway earlier in the day. Nitro growled, drawing my attention to a quad driver I thought was bending down to fix something on his ATV. Looking back I think he could've been scoping out a way to get down to the gardens."

"So it was a quad and not a three-wheeler?"

"Definitely a quad. I didn't spend a lot of time checking it out, because my horse was acting up."

"Have you made enemies of any ranchers? Some cattlemen use all-terrain vehicles during roundups."

"I rarely see any ranchers. I mostly run into their wives at the grocery store or at markets. They're all friendly."

The man put the notebook away again. "I don't like these types of problems in my jurisdiction. Plainly, whoever it is doesn't want to be found. If there's a next time, be sure you tell Dispatch everything. Even if you don't think it's important."

"I will. And thanks for always checking them out. If I've been rude it's only because I'm kind of scared."

He cleared his throat. "My wife tells me she and her friends buy your produce." His phone rang. He took it out of its holder and walked toward his vehicle without looking back.

If he had, he'd have seen Molly's mouth drop open. She hurried into the barn, figuring that was as close to a truce as she'd ever reach with him.

As ADAM DROVE toward the gate he adjusted his side mirror to keep Molly in sight. He couldn't get his mind off her. He hadn't held a woman close in more than two years. He'd taken Diane Tully, Frank's wife, flowers once, and chocolates the next time they'd invited him to dinner—just to prove he hadn't totally lost touch with good manners.

Frank, Diane and their sons had kept him from drowning in sorrow. Thanks to them, little by little he'd forgiven himself for putting money ahead of being a good husband and father.

That regret would always be with him, he thought as the gate swung wide and he drove through. But the awful pain had dimmed. Dimmed enough that he'd begun to feel a spark of romance for Molly McNair.

She'd been soft against his chest. Her hair had felt silky beneath his chin. And even standing in the middle of the fragrant garden, she'd surrounded him with the scent of a woman. How women managed to always smell so fresh and sweet had always been a mystery to Adam.

The gate closed behind the truck and he

lost sight of Molly, who'd linked up with her workers and was going on about her day. Even as he drove to the first of his three market stops for the day, he couldn't stop himself from wondering if she had spent any time reflecting on him as anything other than an employee.

Once he turned off the street and pulled down the alley to the first market, Adam tucked away his vivid memories of Molly and tuned in to his surroundings.

Unlike the old days drilling for oil, or capping burning wells, this job was soothing. On the other hand there was nothing soothing about men who seemed bent on wrecking Molly's business possibly showing up at any time.

Customers were already lined up at the stall. Women with canvas shopping bags grabbed vegetables out of the crates as quickly as Adam off-loaded them from the truck. He picked up the empty crates and collected the money bag. Passing the stall manager a new one, he left for market number two, relieved that the transfers had gone so well his first day on his own.

When he got through the two remaining markets without incident, Adam began to relax. Perhaps the fact that he and Nitro had almost caught the man on the ATV had ended the harassment. He hoped so for Molly's sake.

The rural vet clinic's waiting room was packed at lunchtime. Adam glanced around and had to smile at the variety of animals people held on their laps or had caged at their feet. The usual dogs and cats, but also a hamster, a rooster and a pig. And today, a receptionist slid open a window in a small office Adam didn't recall even having seen at their late-night visit.

"May I help you?" the woman asked.

"I'm here to pick up Molly McNair's dog. We brought him in for surgery last night."

The woman sat and hit a few computer keys. "I see. Yes, he's ready for release. Did you bring a travel carrier?"

"No. I carried him in. He's used to riding in a vehicle without being caged."

The woman pursed her lips. "When an animal has been traumatized, like children, they can act out. And I see on his record he has a collar."

"I'll call his owner. Can you prepare the bill?"

"Dr. Talbot left a note for me to email the charges to Ms. McNair."

Adam shook his head. "I'll pay today," he said firmly. The receptionist nodded.

Outside he dug out his cell. "Molly, Adam. I'm at the clinic to pick up Nitro. The receptionist seems to think I shouldn't take him without a carrier. Do you want me to come back to the ranch for yours?"

"I've…never used a kennel of any kind. I'd ask you to borrow one from Harlan, but all the ones I saw in the hospital were huge. With something that size he'd have to ride outside the cab on the truck bed. Uh, I'm only catching up on computer work. I can ask Henry to watch the office while I run into town to buy a travel carrier."

"Who sells them? I'm closer to town. I'll go buy one."

"There are several pet stores in Laredo." She named two that she'd used, but followed with, "It seems silly to lay out money on a carrier I may never use again."

"Not really. He seemed content in that

cage last night. You may use it to take him outside for fresh air until he's able to run around again."

"True. I hadn't thought of that. All right, get one."

Adam climbed back in the truck. His phone rang again and he saw it was Molly. "Did you forget something?"

"How can you pay for a carrier? It's not a business expense or I'd have you take the money out of one of the market receipt bags."

"I have cash on me. And a credit card. I'll be fine. Don't worry."

"Uh, okay. Get receipts. We'll square away when you get back."

The line went dead again.

Driving to a pet store he found on his phone to be nearby, he ran over how Molly paid her pickers every day and yet worried about every other little business cost. His own business had made gobs of money with every well he and Dave brought in. But Molly had a lot of expenses before deriving any income. That made him wonder how she was really doing.

At the pet store, he chose a fairly large carrier. One that opened wide enough to accommodate a large dog who had to wear a plastic collar.

Across the street from the pet store was a Dodge dealership. He'd been considering selling his bike and buying a pickup. He jogged over to look at one that caught his eye.

Returning to the clinic, he again approached the receptionist. "I have a carrier in my truck," he told her. "It takes up half the cab, so after I settle the bill I'll carry Nitro out."

She passed him the invoice she'd prepared. Adam was startled by the amount. Plainly emergency surgery on an animal was similar to that of a human. An after-hours visit, surgery, antibiotics, plus an overnight stay in the hospital added up.

It made him wish he'd nabbed the idiot responsible. Making him cover this bill and the cost of the plants would be satisfactory retribution.

Nitro appeared delighted to see him. The big dog wiggled all over and licked Adam's hand when he reached inside the cumbersome collar to rub the Dobie's ears.

"I'm surprised to find you still here looking so wide-awake and cheerful," Adam said to Ron Davis, the intern they'd met at midnight the previous night.

The younger man laughed. "It's preparing me to start my own practice. I may buy out a vet in Cotulla so this is good practice. Rural vets get very little sleep."

"I'll bet." Adam extended his hand and the men shook. "Good luck. And thanks for the care you gave Nitro." He bent and, although it wasn't easy, collected the gangly dog. Davis opened a side door and tucked a bottle of antibiotics in Adam's shirt pocket.

Nitro recognized the truck and yipped excitedly. He wasn't as happy over the kennel and tried to scrabble out.

"Hey, behave yourself. I bought you the thickest, softest cushion they had." Adam spent a few minutes letting Nitro get used to his new quarters before driving back to the ranch.

Molly ran out as Adam stepped from the vehicle. "I didn't hear back that you found a carrier. You've been gone so long I was afraid something else had happened."

Adam opened the passenger door and muscled out the big carrier. "I should've called. There was a pickup dealer by the pet store. They have one I like. Once I settle this kennel where you want it, I'm going back there to work a deal."

Molly gaped at him and pulled back from wiggling her fingers through the wire door. "That's a big step, Adam. And a big expense. If I'm poking my nose in it's because I know how much you'll make here after taxes. I point this out because Rick works full-time for me and he was turned down last year when he filed for a loan to buy a car."

"Thanks, but I don't expect it'll be a problem."

A wrinkle formed between her eyes. "Okay, but…" She shrugged. She had no idea how much he earned bartending.

"The Harley was a passing fancy. And with the guys in the SUV still on the loose, and the pair who waylaid me, I'll fare better against them in a pickup than on my bike."

"I'm sorry those jerks are causing problems," Molly said.

"It's okay. Where do you want Nitro? The kennel is heavy."

"Oh, can we put it on one of the flatbed carts so I can move him from the office to the house? I've got an hour yet of input on the computer. The schoolkids will be here soon. And after they leave I'm expecting Tess."

"Will you get a cart?"

"It's in the office."

He carried the kennel into the office and made sure it was secure on the cart.

Molly got on her knees in front of the open kennel door. She glanced up at Adam. "Is he okay?"

Adam handed her the bottle of pills; Nitro looked abject in misery. "Dr. Davis sent these to ward off infection. Nitro's smart, Molly. He's playing you. Reminds me of my daughter. At four, Lindy had to have her appendix out. She perfected big, sad eyes that got her a Popsicle every day." He smiled as he gazed at the dog.

"As competent as you were at the vet, I know you were a good father, Adam."

He stiffened. "No. Back then I was consumed by my work. I like to think if I had the chance of a do-over I'd be better at a lot of things. I know I'd have different priorities."

His eyes had a faraway look, and neither of them spoke.

Finally he shook his head. "Hey, I'm going to take off. Will you program the gate code into my cell phone? If I buy a pickup, I want to be able to get back onto the property! I need to get some clothes, too, and let Frank Tully know I'm staying here for a week or so. If that's okay?"

Molly closed the kennel and stood with a hand up from Adam. "You really don't need to. But, Henry already hooked up a microwave in the tack room. His wife sent a mattress topper to make your cot more comfortable. You guys… I just let you run roughshod over me."

Curving both hands around Molly's face, Adam tipped it up and stared long and hard into her eyes. "I hope you don't really think that. Can you accept that we care about you?"

The expression in her hazel eyes was soft and Adam saw her lips tremble. It was all he could do not to bend to kiss her when she whispered, "Yes...I can."

He slid his hands away, absorbing the tingle in his fingers even after he went out and wrapped both palms around his Harley's handle grips.

He didn't expect to ever fall for any woman again, but, damn, he was.

Falling head over heels.

CHAPTER TEN

BLAST, MOLLY HAD let Adam take off when she'd planned to talk to him about a computer search she'd done on the oil company. It was the same company that had annoyed her dad. People had registered complaints with the Better Business Bureau over as-yet-unresolved pipe leaks. A leak like that could kill a farm.

She had let herself be flustered over Adam's unexpected personal interest. How else could she describe it? His touch lingered on her face...or rather, the memory did. She was finding it difficult to sit at her desk and get back to her spreadsheet.

When she entered the last numbers a few hours later and hit tally it was a shock to see that she hadn't made a profit but instead had again dipped into savings.

She filed the report away and rubbed her

temples as she sat with her elbows on the desk. She shouldn't have ordered the large pecan trees. She had to pay a crew to dig holes today, and another with equipment to plant them tomorrow in the area Henry and Adam had plowed. It was on her schedule to send Rick, Ramon and Adam to pick the trees up from the nursery, but the nursery only guaranteed the trees if they did the planting. And it was too late to cancel the order. The confirmation and final cost had hit her email today. She might yield a small crop of nuts this fall, but probably not until next year—another net negative.

Nitro whined and pawed at his kennel door.

"I'm okay, boy. Just mildly freaked out over money." Getting up, Molly went to his kennel on the utility cart. "Let me get some fresh water."

Taking the bowl she hurried to fill it at the sink at the back of the barn. She had to smile because Adam had left his shaving kit sitting on an orange crate next to the sink. She wondered if he knew how good he looked clean-shaved.

Seeing his kit by the utility sink made her realize the poor guy had no place to shower. And the towels on the nearby rack were thin and tattered. Should she replace them with better ones from her house? He probably wouldn't like being fussed over, she thought as she carried Nitro's bowl back. But she'd do it anyway. After all, Adam had volunteered to protect her. It was the least she could do in return.

She'd barely set the water in the kennel when she was distracted by a screech of brakes outside. Going to the door, she saw the school bus.

She'd forgotten the kids were coming today.

Because she didn't want to leave Nitro alone in the office she went back and pulled his cart outside.

The children piled out of the bus and ran up to her. "What's wrong with your dog?" one boy asked.

Molly didn't want them to know about the damage to their garden so she just told them Nitro had hip surgery.

The kids had been schooled about Nitro's

guard-duty status. But today they gathered around his kennel.

Nitro put his head down and looked sad-eyed. He even turned on his good side and whimpered, which garnered more murmurs from the children.

All in all Molly figured from the way Nitro lapped up the attention, his guard-dog days were over. She smiled and reached her fingers through the kennel squares to rub his foot. "I'll park him in the shade, kids, then we can get started."

Once the cart was situated, several children danced around her. "What are we going to plant today, Ms. Molly?" they chorused.

"First I want you to go down the rows you planted last week. Any weeds you see, pull and drop them in the aisles between rows. Once that's done, collect the weeds in a wagon and haul them to compost bins that sit in back of my house."

One little girl screwed up her face. "What's com…compost?"

"Compost is fertilizer made from natural ingredients such as weeds, grass clippings, twigs and leaves. Fertilizer is food that makes plants grow," Molly said. "Some commercial farms buy manufactured fertilizer. I prefer composting my own."

"My uncle uses cow manure," another girl announced.

"Ugh, that's gross," yet another girl exclaimed. "Manure stinks."

Callie, one of the two teacher-helpers accompanying the group, shushed her. "Devon, let's let Molly tell us more about how she composts."

"I have two types. One is vermicompost with worms using kitchen garbage. The other is outdoor waste. And, Devon, compost only smells if it's not done right."

A little boy snaked up his hand.

Grace, the second teacher, called on him. "Keith, do you have a question?"

"How do weeds grow so fast? We only planted our garden a week ago."

Molly nodded. "Good question. The weed seed may have already been in the plowed ground. Or it may have blown in on the wind. Weeds grow faster than vegetables. Shall we get at pulling them so you'll have time to plant more seed for a winter crop?"

"Why can't we leave the weeds?" This question came from a small girl with a serious face, eyes huge behind round glasses.

"Who knows the answer to that?" Molly tossed the question out.

The children glanced at one another and then to their teachers. "Not being a gardener," Callie said, "I'm not sure, but my guess is the weeds sap nutrients from the good plants."

"Exactly!" Molly beamed. She handed out kid-size rubber gloves. "Some weeds can cause skin rash. Don't touch them with your bare hands. But as soon as the weeds are gone we'll plant new vegetables."

She didn't know why kids loved to plant and pick their harvest, but never liked to weed. She'd always enjoyed the whole process.

The children were good sports and bent to their task. Molly pitched in.

"Okay," she said after they'd hauled the weeds to the compost bins and the kids, especially the boys, inspected the worms. "Now we'll go plant seeds and some bulbs that will produce winter vegetables. When you plan a home garden it's good to always have something in season ripening."

"We planted squash last week. My mom said we only eat that in the winter," Devon piped up.

Molly smiled at her. "The thing about squash is that there are summer squash and winter squash. Last week we planted summer squash." The children listened intently. That was why Molly loved working with third-graders. They were little sponges, soaking in information they'd share with their parents.

"R.J." Molly tapped the freckled nose of a red-haired boy. "Can you and Ms. Grace swing by the barn with me? You can help wheel out the cart of tools and seed." His teacher had told Molly the boy was one of nine children in one of their poorest families. She'd noticed he was always first in line when she gave out free vegetables at school. Now he stood a little straighter at being asked to help.

"What kind of tools?" he asked before they reached the barn.

"Hand trowels like you used last week to dig holes."

"Cool. I can pull the cart, Ms. Molly. I'll be careful to go slow."

"I know. Wait here. I'll bring it out." She opened one of the big double doors and went into the dark interior.

"Somebody's coming," R.J. said as she came out. He pointed toward spirals of dust rising in the distance, inside the entry gate.

Molly passed him the cart handle even as she studied an approaching silver pickup she didn't recognize.

"Why don't you and Ms. Grace take the cart to Ms. Callie?" she murmured. "I'll see who our visitor is and then be out to show you the next step."

The boy hesitated but left with his teacher.

The pickup slowed when it neared the spot where the school bus sat parked with its snoozing driver inside. Molly felt she could rouse the man if the visitor proved to be unwelcome.

Squinting into the sun, she saw the driver's door open and Adam step out. Molly felt her mouth gape even as she shaded her eyes for a closer inspection.

"Hey, how do you like my new wheels?" he called, grinning like one of the school-kids.

It wasn't even so much that the newness of vehicle blew Molly away, but the fact Adam had gotten his hair cut fairly short. Although it still tried to curl over his forehead in an endearing way. He'd also exchanged his scuffed biker boots for fancy cowboy boots, and his scruffy blue jeans for new black ones. And surely that was a black silk tee.

She continued to reel as the kids gathered around and Keith blurted, "It's the guy who had the cool Harley. What did you do with your bike, mister?"

"The salesman at the Dodge dealership bought it. He said he'd wanted one for a long time. We both got what we wanted," he said, patting the pickup.

"Adam! What have you done?" Molly exclaimed as she finally could speak. "It's got to be a thirty-thousand-dollar vehicle."

Adam smiled. "Uh, more like forty. Like

the salesman said, call it king of the road with a Hemi engine. Wait 'til you see the interior. Leather makes it as resilient as a farm truck, but it feels like riding in a luxury car."

Since the children were darting glances between her and Adam, and with Grace and Callie giving him the once-over as if they could eat him, Molly swallowed her shock. Clapping her hands, she got the kids attention. "We don't have time to gawk at Adam's truck. We have vegetables to plant."

They ran back to the garden. Molly trailed more slowly, but noticed the impressionable teachers had hung around asking Adam to see the cab's interior.

He tossed Grace the key and followed Molly.

"What's wrong?" he asked, catching up to her.

"Nothing. I…you caught me off guard."

He frowned. "I told you I planned to buy a pickup."

"Yes, but…" She half turned toward the vehicle and flung out an arm. "I thought. I expected…" She sputtered but failed to complete her sentence.

"Well, that's confusing," he said, plainly teasing her.

She stopped beside the cart, but not before making a cutting motion across her neck. "Okay, kids. Everyone take a trowel. These first three rows we'll be planting red leaf chard. One of you at each end of the row like last week. The next three rows we'll plant these leek bulbs." She held one up.

Devon screwed up her face. "What's a leek? Are they bulbs of water?"

It was Adam who chuckled. "Leeks make a nice taste in potato soup."

"I'm impressed you know that," Molly said. "The other things we're going to plant today are brussels sprouts, and we'll cluster seeds in hills for parsnips. Who here has eaten parsnips?"

None of the children responded. Molly saw Adam wrinkle his nose. "What, you don't like parsnips? They're a great alternative to potatoes."

"My aunt loved them. I prefer cauliflower if I exchange something for potatoes."

"They'll plant cauliflower next month. And spinach."

"Ugh!" Several children made gagging noises.

The teachers had returned and Grace passed Adam back his key. "Listen up, kiddos," she said. "We're here so we'll all learn to eat and enjoy a variety of nutritious vegetables. You're getting this opportunity Molly's offering so you'll harvest foods that supply vitamins and minerals, and give you energy to make you strong. Strong," she repeated, flexing her arm.

"Strong enough to play football?" Keith asked. The others might have teased him because he was the smallest of their group. They didn't. A second thin boy made a muscle with his own skinny arm. "We need to eat everything we're growing, Keith. And I'm gonna tell my brother. He started high school this year, but Coach hardly ever lets Alvin play, 'cause he don't got muscles."

"Doesn't have any muscles, Gerald. 'Don't got' is poor English," Callie said.

Adam picked up a trowel. "Shall we men start at one end of the rows and let you women start at the other?"

The boys all shouted, "Yes," grabbed

trowels and dashed down the rows in the direction Adam had stabbed his finger. They were plainly pleased to be called men.

Molly was grateful to Adam for herding the kids back on track and murmured her thanks.

In a moment of silence that ensued as the girls each collected a trowel and Molly handed out seeds, Nitro began to bark.

Adam's head came up. He swung around until he identified where Molly had parked the dog's cart. "Give me a minute, guys. I bought a box of one of Nitro's favorite snacks, but I left it in the backseat of my pickup."

"I saw it on top of a box sitting next to a duffel bag," Callie said. "I'll go get it," she volunteered. "I had my nails done yesterday. If I garden it'll wreck my gel decals."

"I won't pretend to know what gel decals are," Adam said, tossing her his key ring.

"I'll go," Grace said, intercepting the keys before they reached her coworker. "You supervise the kids, Callie. We wouldn't want you to break an expensive nail opening a box," she said, rolling her eyes at Adam.

Molly might have found the teachers' obvious machinations comical. Except the women were very attractive, and Adam didn't rush to join the boys, but seemed to waste a few minutes watching Grace walk away. Molly felt more than a little disgust.

How could she blame them for fawning over Adam when she found herself sneaking peeks at him? This afternoon he looked so different from the man she'd hired—even different from the man who'd driven off the property a few hours ago.

Not wanting to be caught staring, she knelt to show the girls how deep to dig the holes before dropping in the seeds.

Molly admitted to herself that she'd found Adam intriguing before this metamorphosis. But now he left her heart tripping faster.

Good-looking he was, but if he'd let a car dealer fast-talk him into debt, how reckless was that? Very. She'd come across too many men who needed toys even if it meant putting their families in poverty. That was the reason so many of her female pickers worked two or three jobs. The women were so eaten up by worry it made Molly more determined to subsidize everything she did with cash.

And to be aware of the financial stability of any man she let herself take an interest in.

Where does Adam Hollister fit?

The teacher returned with Nitro's treats. With one eye Molly watched both flirt with Adam when he took the treats to Nitro. On previous trips to the gardens Grace and Callie acted afraid of the Doberman even if Molly had him staked well away from the children. Now the women were too obvious.

She saw Adam motion them to step back before he opened Nitro's kennel to deliver an ear rub prior to dispensing the treats.

Little Leza Novotney stepped between Molly and her view of Adam and his groupies. "How long before what we plant will be ready to cook and eat?" the girl asked.

Molly refocused her attention. "You'll harvest the crops you planted last week by the end of school. What we're planting today will be ready by Thanksgiving after you start fourth grade."

The girl sighed, plainly disappointed.

"That was a big sigh. Are you hungry, Leza?"

"Uh-huh. Mama says we can only have rice and beans for supper until Daddy's unemployment check comes next Friday. Unless he finds a job," she added softly.

Molly took stock of the girl's pinched face and baggy clothes. She knew many kids in the district wore older sibling's hand-me-downs. On her first visit to the school, a teacher had said a local church sponsored a class each year, taking students to a discount store to buy clothes to start school. Some children deliberately chose things too big so they could share with older brothers or sisters. Molly had almost cried when another teacher had commented on three boys in one family who took turns wearing a new pair of shoes they polished every night.

"Ms. Molly, we're finished," Devon said. He and the boy working from the other end stood and removed their gloves.

Adam had gone back to help the last boys finish up. It was well timed, because the bus driver honked his horn, notifying them it was time to leave.

"Those of you who are finished, head for the bus," Callie called. "If anyone's not done, work a little faster. We don't want to keep Leonard waiting."

Jumping up as the children filed past her cart to leave their trowels and rubber gloves, Molly pulled Grace aside. "Can you stall Leonard from leaving long enough for me to pick a bushel or two of corn? Maybe I can talk Adam into pulling enough carrots for all the children to take some home." She quietly relayed Leza's predicament.

"Molly, that's so generous of you. Leza and a couple of others said on the bus that they wished it was Friday so they'd get backpacks of food to take home. Can I help you gather?"

"Thanks, Grace, but I can tell at a glance which ears of corn are ready. You and Callie go ahead and load the kids. Adam and I will pick."

"What are we doing?" Adam asked.

Molly filled him in.

"Poor little tykes. That's awful that they're hungry. Want me to fill one of the crates I set out for tomorrow's pickers?"

"Yes, please. Select the biggest carrots." She started to walk away but Adam caught her arm.

"Do you need me to run to the barn and grab you a crate for the corn?"

"No, but thanks. I set a couple of bushel baskets out here this morning. I'd planned to test the ears in several rows. I know there are enough mature ears to start pickers in the field tomorrow. It will only take me a few minutes to fill two bushels."

Several minutes later they came back together. Adam set down his crate and took both baskets from Molly. "Let's trade. You're huffing like a steam locomotive."

"So...kind...of...you...to...notice."

He slanted her a glance, smiling as he stacked the baskets easily.

At the bus, she handed Callie some brown bags. "Will you see that each child gets a few ears of corn and some carrots?"

The teacher's eyes misted. "Grace told me what you were doing. We rarely meet anyone so generous, Molly."

"If I'd known earlier I could have made

up packs for each of them. On short notice this will have to do."

Leonard took one hand off the steering wheel and reached out to shake Adam's hand when he set the baskets of corn and crate of carrots in the step well. "I see the hunger in some kids' eyes every day when they board the bus for school. Hunger hurts. Too many people don't get that."

Pivoting away, Adam pointed to Molly. "This is the lady who understands and does something about it. Give her the credit."

Molly waved off any notion of credit. "See you next week," she hollered over the children's chatter. To Callie, she said in a lower voice, "I'll see what extra I can pull together for Backpack Friday."

The teacher hugged her.

Adam had already left the bus. Molly stepped down backward to exit and her boot heel caught on the last step, causing her to stumble.

Acting quickly, Adam caught her.

"Call me a klutz," she said, more or less forced to watch the bus depart from within the protective circle of Adam's arms.

"Are you okay? They need to fix a loose rivet on the band holding that step in place. I'm surprised one of the kids hasn't tripped and tumbled out."

"I'm fine. Thank you."

Because Adam didn't seem to feel the need to release her right away, Molly didn't rush it, either. She liked having a minute or two to savor this.

Adam slowly slid his arms away. "How did Nitro fare today?"

"It's odd, but I think him getting hit and having surgery has skewed his ability to act like a guard dog. He let the kids gather around and whimpered as though he wanted to be petted. The way he acts with you."

Adam gave a half laugh. "So it's my fault he likes his ears and belly rubbed?"

"No. It's fine, really. At the time I got him I wasn't working with schoolkids. He's been kind of worrisome around them. You can warn them to stay away, but there're always one or two boys who test the limits."

"I'll have to be your guard dog," he said, a smile kicking up the corners of his mouth.

Molly gave him a light shove, but his grin only widened.

"No, really. Isn't that why I'm staying here?"

"It's one thing to have a dog following me around and quite another to have a grown man at my heels."

"So, put me to work helping out. What's next on your agenda? Do you want me to fetch Nitro?"

"Sure. I have a couple of hours until Tess arrives. I'll do seed-starts in the greenhouse. Then you're free to go."

They still stood where they'd been when the school bus left.

"I volunteered to help, didn't I?"

"Tomorrow around noon, I take delivery of a hundred pecan trees at the site you and Henry plowed. Do you think Nitro will be okay if I leave him alone in the house for a couple of hours to oversee the planting? Before his accident I planned to ride Cappy to the site."

"I'll load Nitro's kennel in my pickup and drive him there. Market deliveries have only been taking me to noon."

"Which is all I'm paying you for, Adam. It's all I can afford," she added, letting out a long sigh.

"I like keeping busy."

She shot an uneasy glance toward his new pickup. "I feel guilty letting you work for free, especially since…well…you went on a wild spending spree. Are you having some midlife crisis?"

His laugh bubbled up from his belly this time. "Are you saying you like the old me better?"

"As if!" She blushed then and stammered, "W-We're eating into my work time. See you at the greenhouse," she said, darting away.

Adam didn't leave immediately. He kept Molly in sight until she entered the barn.

Tucking his hands in his back pockets, he finally turned and slowly walked to Nitro's cart.

Frank had ribbed him about being sweet on Molly. And when Adam hadn't denied it, his friend had asked, "Have you told her why you applied for the job? You should come clean with her. Especially if you're hoping for a real relationship with her."

With his deal off with Dave, though, there was really no reason for Molly to ever know.

Unless, of course, the oil company found a way around her to the land.

Still, he decided as he collected Nitro, Frank didn't know Molly. He didn't know how passionate she was about her farm. And how needlessly revealing the truth to her might be the end of their developing relationship.

And Adam hadn't told his friend how involved he was getting in the farm, too.

He paused to pet the dog. "If I'm not too rusty when it comes to courting a woman," he muttered, "I believe I should stick with my gut feeling and keep that old news to myself for the time being. If there's ever a need to fess up to her," he added, closing the kennel and grasping the cart handle, "I'll be on firmer footing, huh, boy?"

Nitro woofed and Adam took it as total agreement.

CHAPTER ELEVEN

"ONE OF THE teachers told me you have a worm composting station," Adam said to Molly when they were wrist-deep in damp soil they were tamping into small square pots along with seeds.

"I guess you weren't there when I discussed it with the kids." She let some soil filter through her glove. "It's nutrient-rich, so seeds sprout faster and produce healthier plants."

"Interesting."

"Food safety activists pressured Congress to give the FDA authority to enact tougher rules governing noncommercial fertilizers."

"What does that mean for you?" he asked.

"Well, I'm monitoring the situation, as you can imagine. I just got a letter listing all kinds of new restrictions."

"So even though you're using environmentally friendly farming methods, the regulations aren't supporting your work?"

"Support us? Ha. Regulators may soon ban irrigating from open creeks and rivers. I can't afford to irrigate with city water, supposing I was even connected. My house water comes from a well that's not deep enough to water all of my gardens."

"What's their beef with river water?"

"Impurities." Molly planted seeds and set the pots in flats as she talked. "I've installed expensive filters at the point we take in water from the Rio Grande, but there's no guarantee it'll satisfy the next inspector they send out. I'd like to give away more food to poor families, but added regulations usually up my costs."

Adam didn't say anything and she filled the last two crates with the pots then watered them.

"Thanks for your help." She stripped off her gloves. "It's about time for Tess to arrive. Are you sure you won't change your mind and join us for dinner?"

"No, I'm okay. I'll take Nitro up to the

house for you. He's due to have his antibiotic."

"I can administer the pill. I've got these treats he loves that wrap around the pill. He doesn't even know he's taking medication when he eats it."

Nitro roused when they went to his kennel. He gave them such a sad-eyed look Molly tipped her head to Adam's shoulder. He automatically slid his arm around her waist. "I shouldn't have gone out your gate in a rush that night. I feel so bad."

"It wasn't your fault. It was purely an accident." She straightened and pulled away. "A week isn't so long. That's all he has to wear the collar." Molly opened the door and held it so Adam could wheel out the awkward cart.

"Providing no infection sets in. In a week we can take the collar off and he'll be his old self."

They traveled the worn path to the house. Molly ran up the steps, opened the front door and stepped aside, allowing Adam past with the kennel.

"Wow, something smells good in here," he said.

"That's my stew." Molly directed him to set the kennel in a corner of the big kitchen. "You turned down sharing it," she pointed out, picking up the container of pills Adam had given her earlier. "Your loss."

"Maybe I'll change my mind if it's not too late," he said, dropping to his knees to open the cage.

"Really, it's no trouble to add another place at the table."

"Okay, then, if you're sure your friend won't mind."

"I don't know why she would. Tess is the social one of us."

"I'm not the best person to judge social anymore." Adam spent a few minutes petting the dog before Molly popped a treat-wrapped pill in Nitro's mouth.

The surprised dog swallowed it down then licked her hand.

"You traded in your motorcycle and got a haircut. Those are trendy new clothes, too. Usually when someone changes that much all at once there's a reason. You jumping into the social scene?"

Adam took Nitro's water bowl to the sink and filled it. He returned it to the kennel, letting the silence drag between him and Molly.

Her cell phone chimed. Sighing, he stood and stepped out of her way.

"That was Tess," she said. "I released the gate lock and she's coming through."

"Out of curiosity, why do you lock it when anyone can punch the button and drive through?"

"Most cattle ranches operate that way. The fence was only there to keep cattle from wandering off."

"But the whole of your property isn't fenced."

"You mean from the house and barn to the highway?"

"Yes."

"When Dad ran cattle that area was all brush thicket. I had it cleared and plowed for the garden after I came home from Africa. By then Dad was confined to the house. I didn't want to be too far away. I could plant and stay close by."

"Do you agree it needs fencing now?"

The corners of her mouth turned down. "I do, but it's not going to happen any time soon. The pecan trees cost way more than I'd budgeted."

"Then I should install house perimeter motion lights as we discussed the other night. I can check out your wiring now. I'm sure you have some finishing touches to put on the meal."

The doorbell rang. Molly sailed past him and went to greet Tess. She ought to tell Adam she probably couldn't afford to buy motion lights and wire, either. But if he thought she was operating on the razor's edge, he might quit. Funny how not long ago she suggested he do just that. Now the notion was abhorrent.

Flinging open the door, she grabbed for the bread Tess juggled while attempting to untangle her feet and an overnight bag on wheels from her roly-poly dog's leash. "Coco, sit!" Tess ordered the beagle.

From the adjacent room Nitro began barking.

Coco did sit, but not until she'd also circled Molly's ankles with her leather leash.

"I'm afraid to move," Molly said.

Adam stepped behind her and knelt to unwind the lengthy leash.

Tess gaped at the looming man. "Whoa, who is that?" she hissed at Molly, never taking her eyes off Adam. Her fingers went lax and she dropped the handle of her suitcase.

"It's Adam. You guys met. Tess, quit gawking and see to Coco."

Tess dramatically expelled her indrawn breath and winked. "I remember we met. But then you weren't all duded up. Nice transformation, Motorcycle Man, I've gotta say."

"Tess!" Molly admonished.

"Well, it's the truth."

Adam tried to pick up the short-legged, pudgy dog. "Hold still, you little butterball." He unclipped the leash and freed Molly first then Tess. "Quick, close the door or I may lose this little wiggler."

Tess complied and wound the length of chain and leather around the suitcase handle. "Sorry Coco is such a handful. The vet says I should put her on a diet, but I can't bear it. She loves food and she's happy."

"But you care about her health," Molly said.

Caught firmly in Adam's arms, Coco increased the decibel level of her yapping in response to the ruckus Nitro had set up in the kitchen. "I'm going to put her down and let you two sort this out."

"I don't want them racing around. Nitro's only one day out of surgery," Molly said.

"Makes sense to me. Hey, I'm going to grab a flashlight and have a look at the wiring." Adam set Coco down and once she'd scrabbled along the tiled floor disappearing into the kitchen, he skirted the women and went out the front door.

"What's all that about?" Tess took back some of the bread sacks loaded in Molly's arms. "How cozy have you two gotten that you're asking his advice on how to treat your dog? And what's wrong with your wiring? Oh, and where should I leave my suitcase?"

"We're not cozy," Molly said, her chin set stubbornly. "Adam picked Nitro up from the clinic and talked to the vet. And since the incident with the ATVer that I told you about, Henry wants me to fence the garden off from the freeway, which is too costly.

I may plant sunflowers, but Adam thinks he can install perimeter motion detectors."

Tess bobbed her head. "Got it. You covered everything but where I should leave my suitcase. That's unless Mr. Big and Beautiful is sleeping in and I should go home after dinner," she added, giving a teasing wink.

"I swear, you are incorrigible." Molly pointed toward a door to the right of the living room. "Put your suitcase in the guest room. Adam is sleeping in the barn. I did invite him to dinner, though. I feel guilty sending him off to eat a solitary microwave meal in the tack room when he's been nothing but kind and helpful."

Tess wheeled her bag down the hall and set it inside the room Molly had indicated. Hurrying back, she trailed Molly into the well-lit kitchen where the dogs had quieted.

"Look," Molly said, drawing Tess's attention to how their pets sat nose-to-nose, one inside a kennel, the other out, but apparently not knowing what to make of the situation.

"I've seen dogs at my vet's with those collars. That must be hard on them. How long does Nitro have to wear that?" Tess asked.

"A week, with luck. The collar is the worst part." Molly made room on her kitchen counter for the bags of bread. "Dinner's almost ready. I only need to set the table and steam the beans." She washed her hands and turned to Tess. "I think I won't let Nitro out of his kennel until we sit to eat."

They heard scraping noises outside. Molly pulled aside the kitchen curtain and peered out. "That's Adam setting up a ladder by the front door. I hope he knows what he's doing. It wouldn't be fun if we suddenly lost power and had to eat in the dark." She dropped the curtain and made a face.

"Rather that than have him fry himself. And candlelight is romantic, Molly. Hey, point me to the cupboard and I'll set the table," Tess said without missing beat.

"Dishes are in the dining room sideboard. I'll warm the bread. I love the smell of this one you have marked as herb bread. Will it go with plain old country stew?"

"Perfect," Tess called from the next room. "Your dining table is huge for three people."

"I figured on us eating at the table in the kitchen alcove."

Tess appeared in the archway, her hands filled with white ironstone ware. "You don't want to dress a table with a cloth, napkins and center candles to impress you know who?"

Molly slipped the bread into the warming oven. "You are so enjoying heckling me, aren't you? Just set the kitchen table, okay?"

"Actually, I'm jealous," Tess said, stepping around her dog. "I'd love to have a handsome man fall into my lap. And you have one bending over backward to try to please you, and you sound as if you don't care at all."

Molly stood silent for a minute. "Are you saying you want to get married?"

"Of course. Don't you want to share your life with someone? Don't you want babies?"

"After a couple of botched relationships, I try not to hope for those things, but of course I want a husband and babies someday," she said, setting fresh-snapped beans in the steamer.

"Uh, sorry to interrupt," Adam said in a strained voice from the doorway. "I finished checking the wiring. You're good to get motion lights. I can, uh, pick up what we need tomorrow."

Tess didn't seem bothered to think Adam might have overheard their private conversation, but Molly felt her face heat. She fussed with turning on the burner. "We can make a list tomorrow and set a budget, Adam."

Nitro climbed to his feet, fixed his attention on Adam and whined.

"Did you decide against letting him loose to play?" Adam asked, crossing to squat by the kennel.

"I decided to wait until we sat to eat. Both dogs are mooches. I figured they'd be less likely to tear around and more apt to sit quietly under the table."

"Makes sense. I need to wash up. Is there a bathroom down the hall?"

"Second door on your left."

He rose and strode out, taking care not to step on Coco who'd gotten underfoot.

"Sorry if I embarrassed you," Tess said. "I didn't hear him come in from outside, did you?"

"No. Who knows how much of our conversation he heard."

"I'd say enough from the way he looked you over. Now I'm interested in your botched relationships. As in, more than one? You've never mentioned them before."

Molly cast a quick glance over her shoulder at the door where Adam had disappeared a moment before the microwave dinged and shut off. "Shh!"

She slid on oven mitts and lifted out the hot dish. "There's another pair of oven gloves in the drawer next to the stove. Would you grab the bread?"

"It's not going to help to change the subject, Molly."

"I'll tell you later. Who wants to talk about having been dumped?"

Tess had no reply to that for which Molly was glad.

Adam returned to lean his backside on the counter and watch the women bustle around. "I feel bad," he said. "Twice I've come to dinner and both times empty-handed. As a rule I take the hostess wine or flowers."

"I have wine in the cabinet in the dining room. I'll grab a nice Merlot," Molly rushed to say and then escaped before Tess blurted out the question that was in her eyes: What other time had Adam come to dinner? "Wineglasses are over the sink," she sang out from the hall.

"Have a seat," Adam told Tess. "I'll get the glasses." He had them in hand when Molly whipped back in carrying a wine bottle.

"Here, trade you." He delivered a warm, private smile. "I know where you keep the corkscrew." He went straight to the drawer and got it out then made short work of opening the bottle.

Molly placed the glasses and took her seat, well aware of the curious looks Tess was bestowing on her.

Stepping into the alcove, Adam poured. He set the bottle in the center of the table, but didn't sit in the chair Molly indicated. "I'll open Nitro's kennel. We'll see if he comes out. He still doesn't know what to make of that collar."

Molly bent and opened the cage. Nitro didn't come out, but Coco went in and licked Nitro's nose.

Molly laughed. "Sit down, Adam. I'll keep

an eye out to see that Coco stays away from Nitro's bad hip. I'm sure they'll come out in due time."

Adam slipped into the chair at the place Tess had set at the head of the table.

"Hand me your bowls," Molly said. "I'll serve the stew."

Tess passed the salad followed by the vegetable dish and then the bread. Adam was first to speak after they all tucked into their food.

"This stew tastes even better than it smelled," he said after taking several more bites. "That cooker thing seems like the ticket to fixing a meal if you're busy at work all day. I assume stew isn't the only thing you can make in it."

Tess regaled him with meal suggestions.

"They have a lot of slow-cooker recipes available," Molly said, picturing them making meals together.

"If you have a computer you can find all kinds online. Do you like to cook?" Tess asked Adam.

"I wouldn't say I like it." He chuckled, but

smiled at Molly. "Eating out is sometimes a better option for a footloose guy."

Tess studied him. "What did you do before you took the job with Molly?"

It was Molly who answered. "He tended bar. I'm sure I told you. He still works there on weekends. Or he did before Nitro's accident." She turned expectantly to Adam. "You said you planned to let your friend know."

"I did. I help out at Tully's Bar. It's a mile or so outside Catarina. Ever been there? My friend's dad ran it for twenty years. But I meant, have you been to the town?"

Both women shook their heads.

Tess forked up a couple of green beans. "I've always thought bartending required a psychology degree. You read how people spill all their troubles to hairdressers and bartenders."

"Mostly Tully's caters to blue-collar guys stopping off on their way home. Not much need for counseling."

"Uh-huh." Tess stared at him as she chewed.

Adam looked increasingly uncomfortable

and started to eat faster as the silence became drawn out.

"I hate to eat and run," he finally said, "but I don't want to horn in on your evening." He scooted his chair back. "I saved a piece of meat for each of the dogs. Will they eat out of my fingers or do I need to put the meat on napkins?"

Tess grinned, clearly enjoying his discomfort. "If it's food, Coco will scarf it up from anywhere. You can probably tell she loves to eat."

Adam sought Molly's eyes and remained locked on her.

"I'm sure Nitro will eat out of your hand," she said. "I meant it when I said I doubt he'll be a guard dog again. Plus sometimes he seems like more your pet than mine."

Adam didn't deny it.

Coco took the meat and licked his fingers. Nitro shook his head a few times first, attempting to rid himself of the collar. "Sorry, fella," Adam murmured. "A few more days of wearing that thing and then you'll be back to normal."

Nitro took his piece of meat back into his

kennel so Adam went over and closed the door. Smiling at Molly, Adam touched her shoulder. "Thanks for a great meal, the wine and good company. Next time, I'm taking you out." He turned and headed for the hall. "Don't get up. I'll see myself out. And I'll lock the door. I'll also take a jog around the gardens before I turn in for the night. Looks as if it'll be quiet out there, though." He signaled goodbye by touching two fingers to his forehead. "See you in the morning."

Neither of the women spoke until they heard the outer door slam. Tess broke the silence. "That man has got the hots for you, Molly."

The wineglass Molly lifted wobbled in her hand. "Tess, he's an employee."

Tess swirled what was left of her wine. "Don't tell me you didn't see he rarely took his eyes off you. And he wants to take you on a date."

Molly frowned faintly. "He didn't say it was a date. He's a gentleman, and he was offering to pay me back for feeding him a couple of meals is all."

"That man is as interested in being more

than an employee...more than a casual friend, as anyone I've seen."

Molly drained her wine. "I could be interested in him," she said slowly. "He's really nice. And he's been a huge help around the farm. But..."

"What do you know about Adam Hollister? I recall you said he told you his wife and child died. We know he works at a buddy's bar. What else? Is he ex-military?"

"I don't think so. Henry called his references. One was the bar owner. The other was someone Adam had apparently worked for in Dallas. He gave a glowing reference, but Henry said he wasn't specific about what Adam actually did. Oh, one time Adam casually mentioned he had an engineering degree, but he didn't elaborate, and on his application he only wrote 'some college.' Yet for an educated man, who apparently travels, he has limited knowledge about everyday things—like farmers' markets and organic fertilizer. He thinks eggplants are exotic."

Tess sat upright. "Why would an engineer

tend bar and drive truck part-time? Maybe he's a gold digger."

"A what?" Molly set her glass down hard. "Isn't that a term only applied to women?"

"Why wouldn't it fit a man if he's looking for a sugar mama? You're a woman of means. You own a lot of property and a thriving business."

"Tess, that's crazy. You're suggesting Adam's a gigolo."

"Well, if the shoe fits…" Tess's voice trailed off. "I don't want you to be taken in, Molly. I saw you look at him with stars in your eyes, too, girlfriend. And you can't deny the man changed into a hottie in a rapid turnaround. What guy without an agenda does that? Oh, yeah, he's a man on the prowl."

Molly's brow knotted. "He did trade his motorcycle in on a very expensive pickup. A high-end Ram. He said he bought it in Laredo. He used his bike for a down payment, but still, I don't pay him enough to make that kind of payment."

"See. Unless he won the lottery, you need to delve into this further. If you don't want to, I can nose around for you tomorrow. Where did he buy the truck? I'll call and pretend to be his banker or accountant. Just dig a little, if you want me to, that is."

"It feels sneaky. But you've brought up some good points. It'd be hard for me to call his reference in Dallas again to ask for more information. So, sure, Tess, find out anything you can. I admit I'm falling for the guy, okay?"

"I knew it. I hope he's a square shooter, Molly. I want you to be happy. He's a little too old to be trying to find himself. Know what I mean?"

"Yes. I definitely don't need that, Tess. And if he thinks I'll be his bankroll, the man's in for a rude awakening. The truth of the matter is, I'm land poor. After I did some bookkeeping today, I realized I overspent buying pecan trees. I'm still in the red, but at least no one has hijacked Adam and dumped my produce the way it happened to Ramon."

"That's good."

"Yes, but the farm magazine keep running articles about how the FDA is itching to shut down farm-to-fork growers. Something to do with them being the main source of food poisoning, which is ridiculous. But I have an inspection coming up."

Tess watched Molly cork the wine bottle and set it aside. "All I can say is that you have a lot more interesting stuff going on in your life than I do in mine. My nearest neighbor is an eighty-year-old veteran. If Adam doesn't pan out, we need to invest some time in seriously finding other options to meet eligible guys our age. Ones who are gainfully employed."

"Hear, hear!"

They'd just settled into watching a movie when Tess's cell phone rang. Looking annoyed, she set down her mug "Sorry, this looks like business. Can you turn down the sound a minute?" she asked Molly.

"Hello? Yes, this is Tess Warner. You need how many loaves when?" She'd had her feet tucked under her on the couch, but sat up fast, dropping her feet down and almost stepping on Coco. She rubbed away a wrinkle that had formed over the bridge of her nose. "You want six herb, six rosemary and the same number of wheat and marble rye by seven tomorrow morning?" Tess turned her wrist to read her watch.

Molly shut off the movie. She knew when Tess's pleading eyes met hers that her friend intended to leave and fill the order.

Tess said goodbye and immediately got to her feet. "I'm sorry, Molly. That was the owner of a sandwich deli in Pearsall. I contacted them when they opened two months ago to see if I could supply their bread. But they had an in-house baker. He up and quit without giving them time to replace him. They're desperate and offered to pay me double the cost per loaf. If customers are happy with my breads, they may sign on as a steady client."

"No apology necessary. I know they'll love your bread. Let me get Coco's leash."

Nitro started barking and Coco answered back. Molly picked up the little dog.

Tess babbled nonstop on the way out, trailing her overnight bag in her wake. "I hope I can bake all night. I've done it before, but not since I left the chain-store bakery. I don't want a lot of clients who need that much bread, but one or two specialty shops ensures a steady income."

"I understand." At the car, Molly gave Tess a hug. "Call me sometime tomorrow to let me know how it goes. Don't speed going home. Deputy Powell's crew patrols that stretch of highway at night." Smiling, she set Coco in the backseat and closed the door. "Wait, Tess. Remember you have to get out at the gate to punch the opener. Make sure Coco doesn't jump out."

"Right. Will you be all right staying alone? That's why I came over," Tess said, keeping her car door ajar.

Molly studied the dark, silent terrain. "I'll be fine. It's after eleven. There's been no sign of anyone on an ATV." She waved her friend off.

Tess drove away and Molly watched her vehicle's headlights cut through the black night. She was ready to go back inside when she saw lights pop on in the barn. One of the doors flew open and she saw Adam's backlit form.

Was he holding a rifle?

She waved her arms wildly and ran toward

him yelling, "Adam, Adam, don't shoot. Tess had to leave. Stop. It's okay!" She reached him out of breath from her mad dash. Even when she breathed again she couldn't speak.

Adam stood in front of her barefoot and shirtless. And the top button on his jeans was open as if he'd dragged his pants on in haste. His new, shorter hair was standing on end.

"I'd just climbed into bed when I heard tires crunch on gravel. Molly, what's going on? Why are you yelling, 'don't shoot'? Did you see someone with a gun?"

She realized he wasn't holding a rifle but rather a long-handled trowel. The kind the kids had used during the day's planting. "Tess got a call from a client who needs a lot of loaves of bread by morning. She left. No one has a gun. I thought you had one and were running after Tess's car."

He threw his head back and laughed. "Is that why you sounded so panicked? Molly, I don't own a gun. And if I did, I'd never fire blindly at anyone."

He dropped the arm holding the trowel and pulled her into an embrace with his free arm.

"Your heart is beating a hundred miles an hour. Come inside. I'll make coffee. It's plain we're both spooked."

"I left Nitro alone and my house is wide open." Molly didn't think she could sit in the small tack room where the only place to sit would be on Adam's rumpled bed. "I had coffee with Tess. More this late would keep me awake all night. I'm fine. Really. I don't think we've even a cricket stirring tonight."

"All the same, let me put my boots on and walk you back to the house. The barn lights and your porch light don't reach into the shadows."

"Okay." She rubbed away goose bumps from her upper arms as Adam turned. "And maybe put on a shirt," she added feebly, not trusting herself to not throw herself at him in the dark. Oh, she was pathetic.

When he reappeared in a very few minutes, boots on and even a long-sleeved shirt tucked into his jeans, she could only blame her lapse on wishful thinking. Here he was acting like a nice, normal guy while she let her mind run away with her.

He even delivered a very proper, "Good night," at her door.

Molly scrabbled a moment to speak.

Then Adam leaned down and pressed a kiss to her forehead, followed by a second to the tip of her nose. A final one started as a soft brush across her lips. But that kiss went on long enough that she backed through the door he'd somehow reached around her and opened.

She cracked one eye wide enough to see him whirl away, tuck his hands in his pockets and walk off whistling, stopping only to call back, "Lock your door, Molly."

She did, but sagged against it, her mind going blank of every single one of Tess's warnings.

CHAPTER TWELVE

ADAM DIDN'T LOOK BACK. If he did he might return for another kiss. Kissing Molly had been impulse. He hadn't expected to love the feel of her curves and the taste of her lips as much as he had.

It had been years since he'd let himself think of getting close to another woman. More than two because he'd worked abroad for six months prior to Jenny's accident. They'd been married ten years, but for much of their married life he'd worked in Middle Eastern hot spots earning big money, wanting to do right for his family. He'd foolishly thought money would do that.

He'd been twenty-five when he'd met Jennifer. She'd been twenty-three. A part-time model and the only child of wealthy, doting parents.

They hadn't rushed into marriage, maybe

because he was out of the country so much. He'd finally popped the question at twenty-eight, but because Jenny had her heart set on a huge wedding at her family's country club, they hadn't married until the following year.

In hindsight he realized he'd wanted to live up to her parents' expectations. The glitzy wedding they'd insisted on set the stage for their lifestyle as a couple. Jenny had wanted him home more. He should have listened, but his mindset had been all about acquisitions. Big house. Fancy cars. Country club membership.

From birth, Lindy had been his bright spot. Before she could talk he'd Skyped with her and her nanny. They had a nanny because Jennifer had been raised by one. Adam assumed that she, like her mother, wanted to spend her days playing golf and tennis, or meeting friends for lunch or dinner at the club. In fact Jennifer's contacts at the club had netted him Cole, Cole and Stafford, who had helped him incorporate Hollister-Benson Wildcatters.

Kevin Cole had steered him to an investment firm that had made them millions. Dave Benson, too, had benefitted. But Kevin hadn't liked Dave.

Now Adam wondered why.

He hadn't asked.

He had so much to regret...

Taking the last job instead of going home to drive his family to Colorado for Jenny's folks' anniversary. Their fiftieth. A huge deal.

He dropped down on the bed and rubbed his face with his hands. Tonight he'd overheard Molly tell Tess she wanted babies. Not long ago he'd hardly been able to look at a child without grieving for Lindy. But the kids who came to the gardens from the local school had grown on him. It didn't hurt to see them. In fact, he almost looked forward to their arrival.

He laid down and eventually drifted toward sleep, wearing a smile as he pictured what co-parenting with Molly McNair would be like.

Hands-on co-parenting.

Probably even hoeing weeds with a baby in a front-pack.

THE NEXT MORNING Adam skipped breakfast. He got up late and saw that the pickers were hard at work. There were dozens of crates stacked at the end of their rows by the time he emerged from the barn. And he figured Molly had beaten him up and out, too.

"*Buenos días*, sleepyhead," Gena greeted him.

"You should have made more noise out here. I didn't hear my cell phone alarm this morning."

It gave Adam a warm feeling to be teased by one of the workers who'd been standoffish before he'd pulled Bobby Parks from the river. Or maybe Gena had felt more trusting of him after he'd stacked the back of her van with cabbage to hide the mother and her kids.

"Where's Molly?" he asked Carlotta, who set a crate of ripe tomatoes next to where Gena had stacked yellow peppers.

"She, Luisa and Soledad are down in the corn rows. Molly said she'd sent corn home with the schoolkids yesterday. She's showing the others which plants were already picked."

"I don't think I've met Soledad. Is she new?"

Carlotta shook her head. "She comes when she can. Her youngest child has asthma and Soledad can't leave her when she's really sick."

"That's too bad. I don't see Nitro. Did Molly bring him out?"

"Yes. She pulled his cart into the shade of the corn rows. He looks better today. More alert."

"I'm glad to hear that. Well, I'll go bring the truck down and start loading. If Molly emerges and wonders where I am, tell her, please."

Adam hiked off toward where the flatbed was parked.

He drove it down and began loading produce. Crates of corn began appearing at the end of corn rows. And he saw two women hauling them out. Molly remained absent and as the truck bed filled up, he started to wonder if she was avoiding him. Maybe he needed to track her down and apologize for kissing her last night.

Damn, he'd wanted her to have enjoyed the experience as much as he had.

Last night he'd tossed out the idea of taking her to dinner. He'd like to nail that down for this evening, so while delivering in Laredo he could find an appropriate place. He wanted someplace nice with good food, but nothing so ostentatious that would strike him as anyplace Molly wouldn't like.

He was starting to lash down the load when she and the two other workers carried over-full crates of corn up to his pickup area. "Will you have room for these on the truck?" Molly called.

"That puts us heavy on corn," he said, testing one of the straps before jumping to the ground.

Molly set her crate at his feet. "I know, but once we got deep into the corn rows it was evident the ears had ripened fast. Did you see I had the workers each fill a plain, uncolored plastic crate with the vegetable they were picking today?"

"I did. I've grouped them together. I noticed several corn crates you brought up are clear plastic, too. What gives with those?"

"Clear crates get dropped off at the grade school after market. The school address is on your clipboard. Today is Backpack Friday. You can park right outside the office. You'll need to sign in and drop these off after you've completed your regular rounds. Whoever's manning the office will call a custodian to help with a couple of hand trucks."

"Okay. I can stick a hand truck in the cab for good measure."

"Say, I meant to alert you to expect sales at the markets to be down today. This is the last Friday of the month. Money doesn't always stretch this far."

"So there will be more people hanging back waiting for free produce? If that's the case, why don't you send less? You're killing your own profit, Molly."

"Vegetables don't consider profit margins. When they ripen, they ripen. Which is better, letting stuff rot on the vines or giving it away to needy families?"

"I see your point. I suppose there's no way to know when you plant how much will ripen at the end of any given month."

"Correct. There are too many variables, the biggest being the weather. If we have a month of downpours, or an unexpected arctic clipper, I may not have enough to sell."

Adam stroked his chin thoughtfully. "How can you possibly gauge what your farm will earn in a year?"

"Bingo! Farming is so tricky—that's partly why we're losing small farms in this country by the score." She nudged the crate that sat between them. "This year the weather has cooperated to produce a bumper crop of corn. You'd better load up and take off before shoppers spend all their money and leave."

"Roger that."

Adam darted a quick glance around to see which, if any, workers might be near. Seeing they were all trekking toward the barn office where Molly would pay them, he reached for her hand.

"Last night I mentioned, in passing, taking you out for dinner. I know you plan a full afternoon planting pecan trees. Can I assume you'll be tired enough after a busy day to take me up on eating out this evening?"

Molly swayed toward him then seemed to catch herself. "I could be persuaded," she murmured. "Where did you have in mind to go?"

"Do you have a preference? I thought maybe someplace in Laredo."

"Sure. As long as it's not super fancy. I'd be happy going anywhere cowboys go."

Adam laughed. "I would have guessed that. But it is Friday. I noticed at the bar the cowboys wore pressed jeans and white shirts on Friday and Saturday nights."

She matched his laugh. "I can't remember if I did laundry this week. Don't count on me for pressed jeans."

"I'll park Nitro outside the tack room, and come back after I lock the receipts in the office."

"Where's Henry?" Adam asked.

"He asked for today off. Alma's having a couple of moles removed from her back. He's driving her."

"Funny, he didn't mention it to me. I hope the moles are benign." Bending, Adam hoisted the corn crate to the truck. "Do you need me to stick around while you pay the pickers? I notice Henry normally assists with that."

"Only to give him something easy to do, Adam."

"Okay, then. Shall I make dinner reservations for seven-thirty in town?"

Molly halted in her tracks. "We're going to a place that takes reservations?"

"Yeah. I thought I'd choose someplace with a little ambience."

She delivered him an uneasy glance. "Why can't I shake the nagging sense that your idea of 'not fancy' doesn't match mine?"

He waved her off. "Not to worry. I'll promise a place where the candlelight is so low no one will notice your jeans aren't pressed."

She rolled her eyes and went back to the corn rows. A short time later when she returned with Nitro's cart, the Doberman spotted Adam in the back of the truck and started barking.

Adam made a last tug on the final tie-down before jumping to the ground. "Hey, boy," he said, leaning over the kennel. "You're looking a lot feistier today. Don't you think so?" he asked Molly.

"I do. He stood and put weight on that leg a few times when I let him out to eat this morning. And the area that was sutured has no sign of infection."

"That's good. A week isn't really long."

"Says you who doesn't have one of those things around your neck," Molly shot back.

"Right. Maybe tonight I'll wear a tie to dinner. It's the same type of millstone."

Molly waited to head for the barn until after Adam climbed in the cab and started the noisy truck.

Inside the barn, the workers hurried to help her wrest the heavy cart over the door jamb. "Where's Henry?" Carlotta asked.

Surprised the women didn't know Alma Garcia was having minor surgery given the closeness of the neighborhood, she merely said he'd taken the day off. And the women didn't ask any more questions.

She got the cash out of the safe and sat behind the desk. It wasn't long before she'd paid the last worker. Then, because it was the end of the month, she fired up the computer and printed checks for her permanent part-time employees. She put each check in an envelope and taped them to the glass on the office door. The men would drop by at the end of their workday to collect their pay.

Molly realized she hadn't told Adam about this ritual. He hadn't asked about pay. But since she'd see him at the tree planting, she'd give him his check then.

Folding the envelope, she slid it into her back pocket. Even as she posted the amount to her business account she felt guilty knowing he'd spend too much of what little he'd earned here and at the bar on taking her to dinner.

She should have said no.

Except, darn it, she wanted to go out with him, wanted to go out on a real date.

Maybe he had money socked away. It wasn't something a woman asked a man.

Rick and Ramon stopped by to pick up their paychecks. "We set up the overhead irrigation pipes in the area where you had guys with the earth auger dig holes for your orchard," Rick said. "Will you need me to swing by tonight and turn the system on? Or is tomorrow at daylight good to water them?"

Molly shut off her computer before she answered. "Can we draw buckets of water from the system that will be filtered?"

"Yes, if you close the red valve and open the big round one at the base of the main unit. A quarter turn should fill you a bucket."

"Each time I turn it? The nursery guy mentioned putting half a bucketful of water in each hole before they plant a tree. There'll be a hundred."

"You'll need help if you're drawing fifty buckets full of water." Rick frowned. "I have a dentist appointment later today. Ramon?"

He shook his head. "Sorry, if I'd known this morning I could have told my boys to find another ride to their basketball game. My wife volunteered me to drive five kids from the neighborhood to the game this afternoon."

"It's okay. Adam said he'd come see how we're getting along. If he's late popping down there, the nursery guys can carry the water. I'm paying them to plant the trees." Molly checked her watch. "I'd better settle Nitro with food and water, then saddle Cappy and go. I got so involved in bookwork I let time get away."

The sky had turned overcast by the time she rode out. She hadn't watched the morning news, but hoped if a storm was blowing it'd hold off until they finished planting the pecans.

ADAM ROLLED IN at twelve-thirty. He'd told Molly one, but she'd been right about the markets not needing as much produce. The school had been profoundly grateful for Molly's donation. He'd even stopped at a hardware store to buy everything to put motion lights on all four corners of the house and above the double barn doors, and was still early.

The barn was locked and quiet. Nitro roused when he went inside. He took a few minutes to pet the dog. Seeing Cappy was gone out of the corral, Adam decided to phone Molly to tell her about his change in plans so he could stay here and start to work on the lights.

He punched in her number, but instead of her answering, he heard her phone ringing from the depths of the barn.

His heart raced. He ran back toward the stalls, but even as the ringing grew louder, he realized she'd set her cell phone on the ledge above the saddle rack that now sat empty. Obviously she'd saddled Cappy and had forgotten her phone.

It took several seconds after he punched Off on his own phone for his stomach to quit churning and for the blood to quit rushing in his ears.

He pocketed both phones and returned to the front where he carried Nitro's cage out to his vehicle. Then he unloaded all of the electronics and stacked the sacks and boxes in the barn. He had little choice but to drive around to the orchard by way of the river road. He'd made dinner reservations for eight o'clock at an upscale Mexican restaurant highly recommended by Eva and Inarosa. He didn't tell them he was taking their boss out, but they were curious.

He made good time on the freeway, but had to slow down shortly after turning onto the river road. He soon saw that the slow-down was caused by two trucks hauling trees. If he passed them he'd beat them to the orchard. But rather than do that and risk parking his vehicle in their way, he fell back.

The morning sunshine had disappeared. The sky over the river looked murky but Adam didn't think they were in imminent danger of rain.

The big trucks left the highway, taking the rutted but well-worn path Henry had explained had worn down when Molly's dad drove cattle to the river.

Slowing to a snail's pace, Adam noticed an older-model Chevy pickup parked off to the side of the tracks. The lone occupant, a young guy, had turned his vehicle around so he faced the river. Adam figured him for a worker waiting for the trucks to arrive.

He spotted Molly near where she'd tied Cappy to a mesquite by the arroyo separating the pecan orchard from her cabbage patch and cranberry bogs.

Crossing on the sandy soil, he followed

the lead of the waiting worker and backed his pickup around. Shutting off the engine, he honked at Molly, who was loosening Cappy's saddle.

She came straight over, smiling, and met him when he got out of his truck. "You're early. How's Nitro?" Slipping past him, she leaned into the cab and whistled. "You weren't kidding when you said this pickup was like a luxury car inside."

"I'll drive it to dinner tonight and you'll see for yourself." He grinned. "It sits like a leather sofa. I made reservations for eight, but no going to sleep on me."

She didn't ask where they were going. "I've got to show Earl where to park so his crew can plant from both ends of the rows."

"Wait. You left your phone by the stalls. I picked up all the inventory to install the motion lights." He handed her the phone. "If you don't need me here, I thought I'd go back and get it done so they'll be operational by this evening."

She took the phone, but looked a bit shocked. "I didn't realize you were buying the lights so soon."

"Why not? They may come in handy sooner rather than later. I also bought two security cameras we can train on the gardens from the house and barn. If you'd had those, the ATVer might be identified by now."

Molly screwed her lips to one side. "How expensive was everything? You should have given me an estimate first. I don't know if I can afford any of it, let alone extras."

He waved away her concerns. "It's a smart investment, Molly."

"Uh, I'm not sure. But maybe we can return everything for a full refund. Anyway, I need your help hauling water to the holes. Rick and Ramon both had plans for this afternoon."

A man stepped out of one of the trucks and flagged her over. Tossing Adam one last frown followed by a herculean sigh, Molly dashed away.

He hadn't planned for her to pay for any of it, but he didn't know how he was going to make her agree to that.

Adam eased his frustration by muscling Nitro's kennel out of his truck and carrying it over to where Cappy was tied.

He took off his sunglasses, walked back and set them on the dash. He shut the door and gazed around at the workers who emerged from the trucks.

He looked for the lone guy he'd seen, and saw him walking by himself midway down the nearest row of holes. He stood out from the other tree-workers, but Adam couldn't put his finger on why. The guy wore worn blue jeans, scuffed boots, a blue work shirt and a plain blue ball cap worn backward like so many twentysomethings he'd seen frequent Tully's.

Molly was still talking with the older man who was probably the crew foreman. Loping over to where four wiry men lifted trees off one truck, he caught the attention of the nearest one. "What's the guy doing who just flattened himself out next to one of the holes down the row?"

All four men stopped what they were doing and stared in the direction Adam pointed.

"Beats me," the elder of the three answered. "He's not one of Earl's crew. He must work for Ms. McNair."

Adam was pretty sure he didn't. He jogged along the row to find out. Two holes away from where the kid lay on his belly, both his arms in the hole, Adam caught sight of and identified what he'd pulled out.

A probe like the one Adam had used to take the soil samples that had been smashed in his altercation with the two jerks who'd jumped him.

"Hey," he shouted, interrupting the guy in the act of filling the last of three glass vials with loamy earth he'd extracted from deep within the hole. "What do you think you're doing?"

The kid scrambled to his feet and hastened to shorten the probe while at the same time attempting to collect the vials.

He dropped one and knelt to grab it. Panicked, he shoved everything into a small khaki knapsack Adam hadn't seen lying on the ground next to where the guy had been sprawled.

Adam saw the kid gather himself for a getaway. He swung right, then left, clearly not knowing which way to run. Because by then Adam loomed near.

"Drop the knapsack or hand it over." Adam stretched out a hand, but wasn't really surprised when the kid hunched down as if readying himself to make a football tackle. He made a valiant effort to mow Adam down and plow on past him, succeeding in only knocking Adam aside, not off his feet.

Though the guy did his best to flee, Adam, bigger and stronger, made a flying leap and hit the skinnier man at his knees, bringing both of them down with a crash that garnered Molly's attention and that of Earl and his workmen.

Adam heard the glass vials break. He recognized the sound from when the same type of fall had shattered the samples he'd taken. This guy was lucky since the vials weren't stored in his shirt pocket as Adam's had been.

Molly suddenly hovered over them. "Adam, what's going on?"

Getting up, he dusted off the knees of his jeans. "Better ask this guy." Bending and digging under the kid's chest, Adam dragged out the knapsack.

Earl gestured for his crew to go back to

their jobs. "He's not one of my men, Ms. McNair. I'll let you handle this and my crew will start planting. I'll assign two men to fill buckets and pour water in the holes, shall I?"

Continuing to look blankly at the young man on the ground who'd finally managed to sit and hunch over his knees, Molly gave a vague nod to the nursery man. "I saw him drive in, but figured he was on your crew. If not, who is he?"

Adam didn't elaborate for her benefit. He nudged the trespasser with his foot. "I caught you dead to rights taking soil samples, so just confess you were sent here by the oil company."

The kid jerked upright and stared at Adam. "I don't know anything about an oil company."

Adam took a threatening step toward him.

"Honestly! I was standing at a corner with other day workers this morning when a dude signaled me out."

Adam looked at Molly with an eyebrow raised.

"He paid me a hundred-fifty bucks to come here and fill those glass vials with earth I wasn't supposed to touch. All I needed to do was probe deep. He knew holes had already been dug here."

Adam crossed his arms, waiting to hear more.

"Listen, I lost my job at the cannery last week. I've got a wife and four-month-old baby who needs special formula."

"Adam, what's he talking about?"

Adam kicked at the bag. "How were you supposed to get this back to the person who hired you? Did he indicate he worked for an oil company?"

"I can't remember," the kid said miserably. "His name was Dave. He asked me to do this job, paid me and said he'd meet me out at the river road for the knapsack." He lifted his head and scanned the distance nervously.

Adam gazed toward the road, too. He had his answer as to who'd sent the kid.

Reaching out a hand, Adam pulled the young guy up. "Dimes to dollars says the guy who paid you watched through binoculars as all of this went down. In case I'm wrong, I'm going to get in my pickup and follow you out to the road. Don't try to run away from me. I'll have your license plate number and I'll track you down."

"My name is Caleb Cox. I swear if we see the man who hired me, I'll give back his cash." The young man's shoulders slumped.

"Keep the money," Adam said, and then he told Molly he'd be right back.

"You'd better. Who's Dave? What's going on? I don't understand any of this."

At the road, Adam motioned for Caleb to stop. Rolling down his window, he said, "Like I thought, he's cleared out. I doubt you'll see him again, but if you do, let me give you my name and phone number. Tell him to contact me."

Reaching into his glove box, Adam tore off the edge of the sales slip for the Ram, wrote down his cell number and passed it to Caleb, even knowing full well that Dave had his number.

"Do you think he's dangerous?" Caleb asked, fear lurking in his eyes.

Was desperate dangerous?

Adam thought he knew Dave Benson well. Now he wasn't so sure. When they'd parted after Adam dissolved the business on the heels of Jenny and Lindy's deaths, he and Dave were both wealthy. Yet at Dave's last call, and maybe even before when he had stopped at the bar, he'd sounded in need of money.

"I can't swear to that, Caleb. If you know any back roads home, I suggest you take them. And find a new corner to wait for day jobs for a few weeks."

Adam felt sorry for the young family man as he drove off. Turning back to the orchard, he debated what he should say to Molly.

Probably the truth.

Except he didn't know the extent of Dave's involvement with Branchville Oil. They were the most likely culprits behind everything that had happened to Molly. Or was his former partner the one responsible for all of the harassment? Adam needed to know.

He bet he'd soon hear from Dave. Once he had a better idea of his former partner's real role in this mess, he could sit down with Molly and explain everything.

Because the truth was he had fallen in love with her.

CHAPTER THIRTEEN

MOLLY RAN UP to Adam before he could climb out of his pickup. "Where is that guy? He was up to something. Why would you let him leave?"

"He was hired to do a job, and he failed. I had hoped to catch whoever hired him, but there was no sign of anyone waiting up at the road."

She held out the khaki knapsack he'd left behind and shook it under Adam's nose. "What is this weird tool? Earl and his men have never seen anything like it, but there are glass vials filled with dirt. Why would anyone pay to have someone take my dirt?"

"For chemical analysis, Molly. It points to the oil company who thinks there's oil under your land. If an analysis showed likelihood, they'd double down to beg, buy or steal from you in order to drill wells."

Molly pulled back, shock waves wafting off her tense frame. "How do you know that?" she asked, her voice laden with suspicion.

"The kid said he was paid to take untouched earth from deep down. He said the man who hired him knew you had holes dug out here for trees."

"Why come when we're here? He could have done this last night or this morning and I'd be none the wiser."

"I'm only guessing, but probably someone had a mobile chemist waiting nearby, ready to perform an off-site test. If it was positive, no doubt they'd have tried to hustle you into agreeing to sell your mineral rights."

"How many times do I have to turn them down? I did some checking on the internet. Branchville Oil has a lousy record when it comes to pipeline spills. I can't risk contaminants." She tossed the knapsack in the bed of his pickup.

"That's proof they aren't giving up. Don't throw it out, Adam. I want to show it to Deputy Powell."

"Okay."

"It burns me. It's still my land." Molly struck her chest with a fist.

Adam reached out and kneaded the tight cords running from her neck to her shoulders. "Why do you say 'still'? Are you worrying because Dr. Talbot said his friend's land and clinic was usurped by the state?"

Stretching her neck, Molly rolled her head around on her shoulders. "There's that. How much would it take the state to see I'm not making ends meet? I expected my startup costs to be high, but I…oh, heck." She threw up her hands. "I don't know why I'm dumping on you. Are you going to stay and help plant trees?"

Taking a moment to study the crew that had made good progress, Adam pulled Molly into a loose embrace. "I'd rather go back to the house and wire in the lights. I'll feel better taking you out tonight if I know lights will flash on if anyone sneaks around your place. I figure with Nitro inside, he'll bark. And your SUV will be in the driveway. With all that, maybe you can let down and enjoy an evening out."

Molly briefly rested her head on his chest.

"I'd like that. I'm so lucky you came into my life, Adam. You ground me." She breathed deeply, smiled and stepped away.

After she hurried off to check on the workers, it took Adam a few minutes to collect his thoughts. He loaded Nitro's kennel and drove toward the ranch, again staying alert for any sign of a vehicle parked in some obscure spot.

He felt guilty having to wonder if, by applying and taking Molly's job, he'd encouraged Dave to make promises to Branchville he then couldn't deliver.

Adam made it back to the ranch without passing anyone who looked suspicious.

He set Nitro's kennel on the porch, brought the wiring and lights from the barn and set up the ladder. He had lights up on three corners and the camera installed and working on the one that faced the main highway when his phone rang. Tugging it out of his pocket, he teetered on the ladder as he said, "Hello?"

"Suppose you explain why you tackled my man down at the tree site, bro."

"Dave?" Adam set down his tools and

glanced hurriedly around to see if he was being observed. "Don't 'bro' me. What in blazes are you doing? I tried to tell you I'm not going to help you, because you or someone you're working for now sent two roustabouts to beat me up. And Molly McNair is not going to let anyone drill for oil on her property."

"I am taking care of numero uno, good buddy. You screwed me over. You accepted the driver's job I turned you on to and then didn't supply soil samples. And I don't know who told those guys to beat you up."

Adam tried reasoning for old-time's sake. "Molly runs organic gardens, Dave. Just give it up and tell those Branchville yokels to do the same."

"Are you crazy? They've initiated proceedings, and have already had a hearing to go around her and sidestep us. I don't intend to be cut out of the deal. What's wrong with you?"

"What's wrong with you? I'm not having any part of your scheme. I left you a million-dollar company. You should've had more than enough in the bank to live comfortably. Tell Branchville they'll go through me and my lawyers before I let them drill on one speck of Molly's land."

"When you left, none of our former accounts would work with me. Fair warning, Adam. I need that finder's fee and I'm going to play hardball."

"Dave. Dave!" Adam found himself talking to air. As angry as he'd ever been, he sat on the porch and called his old law firm in Dallas.

Kevin Cole was delighted to hear Adam had emerged from his funk and had found a woman he cared for again. "I know quite a bit about Texas eminent domain laws. I'll look into this case ASAP. I told you it was foolish to leave your company and your good reputation in Dave's hands. Just so you know, he was in Macau last year gambling with some big players."

"That would explain why he needs money. Speaking of which, let me give you my credit card info."

"Don't worry about fronting funds. I'll set you up on a retainer. How badly do you want to win this, Adam?"

"I want Branchville Oil and Dave Benson, and anyone else, off Molly McNair's back."

Kevin took Adam's cell number and his address at Frank Tully's, and promised to be in touch.

Relieved, Adam gave Nitro a treat, moved his ladder and got back to work.

He was finishing up installing the second camera over the barn door in evening shadows when Molly rode in.

"I'm impressed," she called, swinging out of the saddle. "I rode past the side of the house and both front and back lights kicked on, lighting the area all the way to the corral."

Her arrival also triggered the motion light above where Adam worked, leaving him and Molly in a large pool of golden light. "Give me a few seconds and I'll check to see if you show up in a photo on this camera." He snipped a wire, scraped it bare and deftly twisted it with another. He quickly wrapped the spot in black electrical tape from a roll pulled from his shirt pocket.

Molly stood below holding Cappy's reins. "There's a camera up there? I don't see it."

Adam laughed. "That's the objective. It's supposed to secretly capture you."

"Oh. Has it done that already?"

"Doubtful. We need to step outside the lighted area long enough for it to turn off. Then if we set it off again it should take a photo."

"So it will snap a picture of everyone who goes in and out all day long? Seems like a waste of film or tape, whatever."

"It's digital. Last person out for the night should set the system. There's a keypad inside the barn. For the house it's beside your front door."

"High-tech. Now if this low-tech person can remember to set it, all will be well."

Adam climbed off the ladder. He set it down, then took Molly's arm and moved them and the horse a few feet away. The light went out. He placed his hand on her waist and stepped forward until the light sprang to life again. "You go on and take care of Cappy. I'll remove the chip and make sure it fired. For now the reader is in the tack room. Later you can find a place for it in the office."

"What is the code I use to set the system?"

He grinned. "Garden. You can change it if you'd like." Resetting the ladder, he climbed up and removed the thumb-size chip and climbed down again.

"I ought to be able to remember that." She rolled her eyes and led the horse toward the corral. Stopping, she glanced back. "Are we still going to dinner?"

"Reservations in downtown Laredo at eight. You asked for casual. The people who recommended the place promised good food country style."

"Good. I'm hungry, but too tired to do much but shower and get into comfy clothes."

Adam looked at his watch. "I'll drive up to collect you in half an hour. By the way... that keypad is coded. Guard dog."

"HAVING DINNER OUT is such a treat," Molly said forty minutes later as she sank into the plump leather bucket seat of Adam's new pickup. "I can't even remember the last time I went out."

"You work too much. You need to schedule some time for yourself."

Molly worried her lower lip. "I need to do more of the work myself. I'm already losing the battle to make the gardens pay."

"Shake off the worry for tonight. I want you to enjoy yourself."

"What shall we talk about, then? I'm afraid running the gardens is all I know."

He punched a button and country music wailed from the speakers. "Lean back, relax and listen to the music. We can talk later."

She took him at his word. As Tim McGraw morphed into Luke Bryan to Carrie Underwood, Adam thought maybe she'd fallen asleep. But when he parked outside the restaurant, she opened her eyes and her lips curved in a smile that made him suck in a sharp breath and picture waking up to that smile every morning. "We're here," he said inanely.

"Are you sure? It looks like a warehouse district."

He turned the direction she was looking and panicked. Then a couple emerged from a weathered wood door and Adam heard laughter and mariachi music until the door shut behind the departing couple. "Let's go see."

He sped around the hood to assist Molly out, guiding her through the darkness with a hand at her waist. There wasn't a name over the door, only a street address. But once they went inside the area opened up to secluded tables set with miniature lanterns, and a hostess stepped up to greet them.

"Adam, I love Mexican food. You couldn't have picked a better spot."

The knot that had gripped Adam's stomach when he thought the women at the market had steered him wrong, loosened. After they were seated, he took Molly's hand across the table. "I'd like this to be the first of many evenings out for us."

"I can't spare many hours away from the farm."

The waitress brought menus and they fell silent to study them. Molly suddenly leaned across her menu to whisper loudly at him, "Adam, I forgot to give you your paycheck for the month. We should make an excuse and go. The price of these meals won't leave you anything to live on."

He chuckled. "Don't worry. I'm not broke. Order anything you want. I wasn't kidding when I said I want this to be the first of many nights we go out, Molly. I actually want more than just going out."

"Wh...at?" She looked up.

"I...ah...don't want to rush you, but we aren't kids. I know what I want long-term. You're it, Molly. I hope you feel the same way."

Her mouth flopped open, but the waitress came to take their orders. Molly managed to stammer hers out. The minute the waitress left, she collected her purse and rose. "Excuse me a minute. I need to run to the ladies' room."

Adam half rose, intending to assist her out of her seat, but she fled and he sat again, worried that he may have spoken too hastily. Maybe she didn't see him as a husband or a partner for life. He'd been in a rush because he suddenly felt life passing him by. And he wanted to protect her.

In the lounge, Molly pulled out her phone.

She punched in Tess's number. "Hi, it's Molly. Tess, did you call the car dealer to see if you could learn what kind of terms Adam signed up for in buying that expensive pickup?"

"Sorry, Molly, I didn't. The bread order took all of my time. Are you okay?"

"I'm out to dinner with Adam. The place he took me looks as if it should be a mom-and-pop restaurant. But it's exclusive, and pricey. And he started the evening saying he wants more than dating. He said I'm everything he wants. It came out of the blue. And Tess, maybe he is what you said. A gold digger. My land is worth a lot."

"If he's paying, what have you got to lose? Don't freak out. I promise I'll make that call in the morning."

"Okay. Good. I'll try to just enjoy my meal." Molly put her phone back in her purse, fluffed her hair and rejoined Adam.

"Hey, I didn't mean to shock you," he said. "I ordered sangria. Let's relax tonight."

Their piping-hot meals arrived and Adam asked Molly about the years she'd spent in the Peace Corps. He seemed genuinely interested in what she'd done. And because she'd taught farming in remote villages, talk turned to her decision to turn her father's ranch into organic gardens.

"I'm not in a good spot to market to celebrity chefs," she said. "Not like in LA or San Francisco. But I see a place like this buying fresh produce. If I found enough high-end consumers, I could still afford to sell cheaply at local markets and do charity work with the schools. Farmers' markets may not sustain my costs."

"It sounds to me that if you had a choice, helping poor families eat better would be your top priority."

"Of course, but like I said, every month I'm eroding my nest egg."

"Have you thought of incorporating your farm as a charity? You might be able to expand what you do with the backpacks to other area schools."

"I'd like nothing better, but charities need funding." She stifled a yawn.

"You're tired," Adam noted, signaling for the check. "We'll have to talk more about how you might qualify for government grants, or others ways you could generate backing."

She sat and tried to comprehend how he pulled out a money clip and peeled off several bills he tucked into the folder with the bill. He didn't wait for change, but stood and escorted her out. Molly was so tired and befuddled she fell asleep on the drive home.

Light awakened her with a start. She realized Adam had parked in front of her house and the light fell from her new motion detectors. Covering another sleepy yawn with her hand, she smiled sheepishly at him. "You probably aren't used to taking a woman out for a lovely dinner and having her fall asleep on you."

He left his vehicle's engine running, but slid out of his seat and went around to open her door. "I need to find a way to do more of your chores so you have more energy to go out for fun. You were too zonked to see that everything looks quiet around the gardens. No mischief tonight." He walked her to the door and they heard Nitro barking.

"Are you awake enough to remember how to reset the perimeter lights after you go inside?" he teased, swiping a finger lightly down her nose.

She bantered back. "It'd be hard to forget 'guard dog.'"

Then he kissed her and Molly's mind went blank. She hung on to his shirt for support and in the process dropped her purse.

He released her and scooped it up. Taking out her house key, he unlocked her door. Putting everything back in her hand, he dusted a thumb across her lips. "Off to bed with you," he murmured in a sexy, sleepy voice. "Dream about me and some of the things I said tonight."

He bounded down the steps, climbed into his pickup and, after she went inside, he drove to the barn.

Molly wasn't sure she could breathe, let alone dream. But as she stumbled around getting ready for bed, her mind floated on clouds of pleasure imagining what it'd be like to have Adam Hollister in her life forever.

ADAM WOKE UP to a fierce pounding at his door. He'd spent half the night on his laptop trying to find information on how to form a charitable organization, and he was still bleary-eyed. He started to get up when his door flew open and Molly stepped inside shaking papers in his face.

Her eyes were so bright with fury he almost couldn't think fast enough to drag the crumpled sheet over his nakedness.

"What in the...?"

"Don't. Don't say one word, you lying, sneaking, silver-tongued wildcatter!"

She flung one piece of paper she held after another. "That email is from your partner, Dave Benson. He kindly provided internet addresses so I could read about all of your many exploits bringing in oil wells for sheikhs and kings all over the world. He also said you applied for my truck driver's job to take earth samples for Branchville Oil."

"Molly. That is why I originally applied for the job. But it wasn't long before I was on your side."

"Oh, stop! This email is from the county court. Because my dad and I rejected Branchville Oil's offer, they petitioned the state to take part, if not all, of my land for the bogus reason that their oil well will provide wage earners in this area high-paying jobs. People like you and your friend don't care what happens to the planet or the poor, all you want is to burn every last drop of fossil fuel."

She threw that paper at Adam's face, making him duck.

"I want you packed up and gone from here in fifteen minutes. And I don't want to ever see you set foot on McNair Gardens as long as it remains mine." Giant tears rolled down her face.

"Please don't cry. I swear to you, Dave is mad because I told him to get lost. Give me a minute to dress. Then we can sit down and discuss this rationally."

"No. Frankly my rage tastes better. Any talking I do from now on to you oil people will be through Gordon Loomis, my lawyer." She turned and fled, slamming the door behind her so hard it bounced open again.

Adam spent a moment being so angry at Dave Benson he could've wrung his neck. As he dressed he calmed slightly. Enough to figure packing and leaving temporarily was his best avenue.

It didn't take him long to stuff everything he wasn't wearing into his duffel bag.

Striding down the hall he saw Molly seated in her office behind her desk. She had her face buried in her hands. Nitro's kennel sat on his cart outside the door. Adam bent and patted the whining dog. He straightened and tried the office door.

On finding it locked, he rapped on the glass. "Molly, hear me out, please. I've fallen in love with you. I believe in what you're doing here. I'd never do anything to hurt you."

She uncovered her face. Then she clapped both hands over her ears and closed her eyes.

Adam heard the vehicles of the pickers pulling in. Blowing out a frustrated sigh, he picked up his duffel and left.

CHAPTER FOURTEEN

A MONTH AFTER Molly tossed Adam Hollister off her farm, she sat in the office of Gordon Loomis, listening to her family's longtime attorney natter on.

"It's true, Molly. Three weeks ago, I was paid a surprise visit by a Dallas lawyer, Kevin Cole, from Cole, Cole and Stafford. I checked them out. They have one of the best reputations in the state for winning land acquisition cases. They do more, of course. They're a full-service law firm. But some attorneys, when they get famous, take on pet projects. This guy offered his assistance pro bono. I told you I've never argued against the state before. Frankly I don't think you have anything to lose in accepting their help."

"Only land that's been in my family for generations," she said glumly, but thought the name Kevin Cole sounded vaguely familiar. Except she didn't know anyone in Dallas. All she'd ever done was change planes there.

"I can see you're distressed. Have you heard anything I said about what I learned from Mr. Cole?"

"Probably not, Gordon. I'm nervous about going to court today. My friend, Tess, said I should wear a navy-blue suit so I look demure but professional. I had to spend money I don't have on a suit I'll never wear again"

"You look fine. Lovely." The elderly lawyer rose, shut and picked up his briefcase. "I'll drive us and fill you in on how Cole plans to plead our defense. You need to be up to snuff in case the judge asks you questions."

Happy for his offer, Molly followed him out and climbed into Gordon's older-model luxury Lincoln. It sort of reminded her of Adam's pickup interior, making her more glum. Far too many things reminded her of Adam.

"As I attempted to explain earlier," Gordon said, merging with traffic on the freeway, "Cole is bringing papers that will make

McNair Gardens a philanthropic foundation. He, his partners and I will be listed as board members. You will be sole proprietor. You just need to sign multiple copies, including a set he'll give to the judge."

"A foundation?" Molly sat forward and frowned at Loomis. "How does a foundation in name only work? I doubt the state, or Branchville Oil, has lawyers who'll be easily hoodwinked."

"Cole promised it's legitimate. He has a wealthy donor willing to back this type of charity. One providing produce to underprivileged families."

The term "charity" caused something to go *ding, ding, ding* in Molly's brain. At dinner with Adam, before she'd learned what a rat he was, he'd asked if she had ever considered making her farm a charity. Now, bringing up Adam's name only made her heart ache.

He'd left the day she'd ordered him off her property. She hadn't heard boo from him since. Many times she'd considered phoning him. Because, among other things, after it came to light he'd paid for Nitro's surgery and the motion lights he'd installed for her safety, she needed to thank him.

She couldn't even bring herself to advertise for another driver even though Henry insisted she should.

Everyone missed Adam, including Nitro. But no one as much as her.

"You're not going to faint, are you?" Gordon asked, pulling into the parking lot that served the Webb County Courthouse. "You've gone pale."

"Gordon, I don't understand. Who would underwrite someone like me, trusting me to carry out the work of a charitable foundation, without first visiting my farm?"

The lawyer shrugged. "I'm sure Mr. Cole can give you the particulars. He said the man was a multimillionaire. People with that kind of money are eccentric. It's probably someone with people who can find out what a good person you are. And capable."

Adam thought she was capable. But he was still bartending for his friend and living in a trailer.

She had wasted one evening driving to the bar. Then she'd lost her nerve and hadn't gone in. Maybe if Tess had gone along she would've had the courage. But Molly didn't want her friend to call her pitiful for hankering after a guy who'd done her dirt—someone who found her so forgettable. Obviously his claim that he loved her had been a lie.

She left the car and straightened her skirt. Tess had said she needed to wear heels. Those, too, were foreign. Molly hoped she didn't wobble when she hurried to catch up to Gordon.

He knew where the courtroom was. They went in and she looked around at the brass fixtures and the Mediterranean-tile floors as he spoke to the clerk. There were four portly men in suits seated at one table below the judge's bench. A younger man sat alone at the second table. Molly caught him watching her and she ran a nervous hand up the leather handle of her shoulder bag. He had dark hair and marble-hard eyes.

Gordon beckoned her. Looking neither right nor left, Molly took care to step carefully so as not to slip and fall on the slick floor.

"I'm Kevin Cole." The man who'd eyed

her with such intensity stood and clasped her cold hand. Then he slapped Gordon on the back and pulled out two of the remaining three chairs. "Did Gordon explain I need you to sign papers declaring your farm a philanthropic foundation, Ms. McNair?"

"Yes, but I'm still skeptical."

"I believe it'll save your farm. You want that, don't you?"

"Of course," Molly hastened to say. "But isn't it highly unusual?"

"Not really." The younger attorney separated several sets of pages and held out a gold pen. "The court will be called to order shortly. Sign these, please. I have to take a copy to our opposition and see that one gets to the judge."

She had tons more questions and no time to ask them or read the fine print. But, as Gordon had said, why wouldn't she accept help to keep her farm? He seemed convinced this was the right move and her dad had trusted him for years. Maybe this last-ditch effort wouldn't work. But maybe it would. She signed five forms and passed back his pen. He put the sets in empty folders, gave her one and Gordon another. Then he got up and took a step toward the opposition's table.

Molly watched him until the door they'd come through opened and closed. She glanced around then, but couldn't see past Gordon's wide body.

Kevin Cole turned back and leaned down. "Did Gordon remind you to silence your cell phone?"

"Uh, no." Watching him stride away again, Molly opened her purse and dug out her phone, putting it on mute.

Cole had no more than returned from giving the clerk a folder than she asked everyone to rise for the judge.

Molly saw a diminutive woman in crisp black robes enter, take a packet from the clerk and then step up behind the bench. Apparently the men at the other table had hoped for a different judge.

She heard a flutter of papers and a plethora of hushed murmurs, and wanted to ask Kevin or Gordon what that was about; however the judge put on her glasses, opened the file and leafed through several pages as the clerk stated the case and what Molly's team was countering. An unobtrusive court reporter typed away.

The judge gazed over top of her glasses. "Mr. Graybill. I see you want the state to appropriate Ms. McNair's farm today, because this is the last day the federal government will give your company matching funds to drill for oil there."

"Yes, Your Honor." A beefy man at the other table jumped up. "You'll see a report from Branchville Oil's chemist noting all signs point to a pocket of oil running from one edge of the farm to the other. Given the breadth of it, they could produce as much oil as we've taken from the Permian Basin in three years."

"Could?" the judge said sharply. "I see nothing here proving anyone has actually found shale deposits beneath the gardens. Land that's fully *planted.*" She stressed the word.

"No, Your Honor. Ms. McNair's father ordered my clients off his land before our tests were conclusive. Michael McNair was dying of cancer. My client wanted to be respectful, so didn't press the point with Mr. McNair's daughter."

Molly snorted, then when Gordon jabbed her in the ribs, covered it with a cough.

The judge turned her gaze on them. "Mr. Cole. I see you've flown in from Dallas to represent Ms. McNair. Why?"

"I have a long-standing client who likes that the farm is serving low-income families, and is teaching local children to grow and eat nutritious foods. With our client's generous backing, Ms. McNair can expand her program and put more food into area schools' Friday backpack programs. Those go home to feed schoolkids and their families on weekends. Organic gardening and oil aren't a good mix, Your Honor."

The judge paged through the folder Cole had given her clerk. "I'm aware of the food program. I assume your client is here to vouch for what you say—his willingness to invest at least one million dollars? I see verification from his bank that he has more than has enough funds. I'd like to hear him swear to the court that he's in for the long haul."

"I am, Your Honor." Adam Hollister got up from a chair on the other side of Gordon Loomis.

Molly almost fell out of her seat. She might have if Kevin Cole hadn't steadied her and murmured, "Shh."

A lump filled her throat. She had thought Adam looked fantastic in jeans and a T-shirt. In a three-piece-suit, he was devastating. She almost missed the fact he was swearing to the judge that he'd helped with her gardens, had met many of the people she served and, yes, had the money to fund a foundation.

"I met the children and their teachers. I can attest to the fact there's a great need for good food in the homes of their struggling families. Anyone who shops at a farmers' market knows how important they are to their community. I will back Ms. McNair for as long as she needs me to."

"I'm familiar with that area of Texas," the judge said. "Mr. Cole, I see you've provided notarized statements from school principals who speak highly of Ms. McNair's generosity. All say they need more farmers like her. I checked out the farm bureau's statistics. Southwest area crops have seen a ten to twenty percent drop in yield due to increased construction of oil sites. There are enlightening documents from the Better Business Bureau that point to Branchville Oil's lax cleanup record."

The other lawyer broke in to say the complaints were overblown.

"You're out of order."

The judge perused more papers then looked over her glasses at both assembled teams.

"The fact is, for a state to take privately owned land for oil or gas exploration there has to be need. In other words, a shortage. Research shows that doesn't currently exist." Removing her glasses, she closed the file. "Texas or the greater US does not need Ms. Molly McNair's organic farm. I'm ruling in her favor. This court is adjourned."

She struck her gavel then stood.

In stunned silence the plaintiffs and defendants scrambled to their feet even as the judge bustled out.

The group from Branchville shouted objections, but the black-robed woman didn't hear because the door closed behind her.

Huffily gathering their briefcases, the men representing the oil company stalked from the room.

Molly tried unsuccessfully to blink away the tears clouding her vision even as she tried to assess everything that had just transpired.

Kevin Cole and Gordon Loomis shut their briefcases and talked amicably as they walked to the door.

Belatedly, Molly scrambled to pick up the folder and her purse.

Adam leaned over. Using his thumbs, he whisked away her tears. "The farm is out of danger."

"Is it for real or a sham?"

"It's real."

"Why didn't you tell me? Clue me in before this? I'm so mad at you, Adam Hollister."

"I wanted to many times, but I honestly didn't know how. I fell in love with you and that made all the difference."

She snuffled and rubbed her nose with the back of her hand.

He handed her a tissue then brushed a kiss on her trembling lips. "I wanted to tell you I made a fortune wildcatting. I was afraid you'd react exactly the way you did when you found out. Dave Benson and I each banked a ton of money. I lost my family and I didn't want my money. But after meeting you I learned there's so much good can be done with it. I like what you're doing. I like helping you. I tried to tell you I fell in love with you, Molly. That hasn't changed."

She melted under the earnestness in his gray-blue eyes. "I've missed you. Not only all you did around the farm, but you. I drove to Tully's bar to ask you to come back, but I chickened out. Please, can we start over?"

"Nothing would please me more. Let's not waste any more time. Since we're both here at the courthouse, let's go downstairs to the registrar and file for a wedding license. We wouldn't have to use it right away, but—"

Molly smiled a wide smile and broke in, "I know…we're neither one getting any younger. You said that once. Can we have a fall wedding at the farm? Maybe a community barbecue like my dad held at the end of his roundups?"

"Whatever you want. By the way," he said, "Kevin hired a private detective who learned a Branchville executive hired the men who attacked Ramon and me. Dave told them he was wheeling and dealing with you. They really saw me as no more than another driver-helper. Their aim was to make you vulnerable enough to sell to them. Kevin gave the evidence to Deputy Powell, who promised to make arrests."

"Adam, that's fantastic news. Now I won't have to take Nitro back to remedial guard-dog class." She touched a finger to Adam's lips.

He took it as an invitation to kiss her. They kissed until the court clerk interrupted. "Uh, folks, you may want to clear the court-room. We've got another case due shortly."

"Give us one minute." Loosening his tie, Adam dug in his pocket and brought out a ring with a green center stone. "I bought a green diamond for a lady who has a green thumb."

Molly's eyes widened as he slipped the ring on her finger. "Oh, Adam, it's perfect. How did you…? I love you, too. Yes, let's go get that license."

He slung an arm around her shoulders, helped her rise and propelled her to where the two attorneys waited by the door.

"Hold on." Molly reached down and slipped off her high heels. "Just so you know, you proposed marriage to a country farm girl. Don't expect a glamorous wedding or anything."

"Amen to that," Adam said and then prevailed on their respective lawyers to serve as witnesses at their wedding, which both gladly agreed to do.

"Your dad would be pleased," Gordon said. "He offered a toast at the end of every roundup. 'All's well that ends well.'"

* * * * *

REQUEST YOUR FREE BOOKS!
2 FREE WHOLESOME ROMANCE NOVELS IN LARGER PRINT
PLUS 2
FREE
MYSTERY GIFTS

⋇⋇⋇⋇⋇⋇⋇⋇⋇⋇⋇⋇⋇⋇⋇⋇⋇⋇⋇⋇⋇⋇⋇⋇⋇⋇

HEARTWARMING™

⋇⋇⋇⋇⋇⋇⋇⋇⋇⋇⋇⋇⋇⋇⋇⋇⋇⋇⋇⋇⋇⋇⋇⋇⋇⋇

Wholesome, tender romances

YES! Please send me 2 FREE Harlequin® Heartwarming Larger-Print novels and my 2 FREE mystery gifts (gifts worth about $10). After receiving them, if I don't wish to receive any more books, I can return the shipping statement marked "cancel." If I don't cancel, I will receive 4 brand-new larger-print novels every month and be billed just $5.24 per book in the U.S. or $5.99 per book in Canada. That's a savings of at least 19% off the cover price. It's quite a bargain! Shipping and handling is just 50¢ per book in the U.S. and 75¢ per book in Canada.* I understand that accepting the 2 free books and gifts places me under no obligation to buy anything. I can always return a shipment and cancel at any time. Even if I never buy another book, the two free books and gifts are mine to keep forever.

161/361 IDN GHX2

Name _____ (PLEASE PRINT) _____

Address _____ Apt. #

City _____ State/Prov. _____ Zip/Postal Code

Signature (if under 18, a parent or guardian must sign)

Mail to the **Reader Service:**
IN U.S.A.: P.O. Box 1867, Buffalo, NY 14240-1867
IN CANADA: P.O. Box 609, Fort Erie, Ontario L2A 5X3

* Terms and prices subject to change without notice. Prices do not include applicable taxes. Sales tax applicable in N.Y. Canadian residents will be charged applicable taxes. Offer not valid in Quebec. This offer is limited to one order per household. Not valid for current subscribers to Harlequin Heartwarming larger-print books. All orders subject to credit approval. Credit or debit balances in a customer's account(s) may be offset by any other outstanding balance owed by or to the customer. Please allow 4 to 6 weeks for delivery. Offer available while quantities last.

Your Privacy—The Reader Service is committed to protecting your privacy. Our Privacy Policy is available online at www.ReaderService.com or upon request from the Reader Service.

We make a portion of our mailing list available to reputable third parties that offer products we believe may interest you. If you prefer that we not exchange your name with third parties, or if you wish to clarify or modify your communication preferences, please visit us at www.ReaderService.com/consumerchoice or write to us at Reader Service Preference Service, P.O. Box 9062, Buffalo, NY 14240-9062. Include your complete name and address.

HW15

LARGER-PRINT BOOKS!

**GET 2 FREE
LARGER-PRINT NOVELS
PLUS 2 FREE
MYSTERY GIFTS**

Love Inspired®

Larger-print novels are now available...

LILP15